THE SHOOTING SCRIPT

IN GOOD COMPANY

IN GOOD COMPANY

SCREENPLAY AND INTRODUCTION BY
PAUL WEITZ

A Newmarket Shooting Script® Series Book
NEWMARKET PRESS • NEW YORK

This book is published simultaneously in the United States of America and in Canada.

FIRST EDITION

10 9 8 7 6 5 4 3 2 1

ISBN: 1-55704-672-7

Library of Congress Catalog-in-Publication Data
Weitz, Paul.
In good company : the shooting script / screenplay and introduction by Paul Weitz — 1st ed.
p. cm. — (A Newmarket shooting script series book)
Includes bibliographical references.
ISBN 1-55704-672-7 (pbk. : alk. paper)
I. In good company (Motion picture) II. Title. III. Series.
PN1997.2.I54 2005
791.43'72—dc22 2004027766

QUANTITY PURCHASES
Companies, professional groups, clubs, and other organizations may qualify for special terms when ordering quantities of this title. For information, write to Special Sales, Newmarket Press, 18 East 48th Street, New York, NY 10017; call (212) 832-3575 or 1-800-669-3903; FAX (212) 832-3629; or e-mail mailbox@newmarketpress.com.

Website: www.newmarketpress.com

Manufactured in the United States of America.

OTHER BOOKS IN THE NEWMARKET SHOOTING SCRIPT® SERIES INCLUDE:

About a Boy: The Shooting Script
Adaptation: The Shooting Script
The Age of Innocence: The Shooting Script
American Beauty: The Shooting Script
Ararat: The Shooting Script
A Beautiful Mind: The Shooting Script
Big Fish: The Shooting Script
The Birdcage: The Shooting Script
Blackhawk Down: The Shooting Script
Cast Away: The Shooting Script
Dead Man Walking: The Shooting Script
Dreamcatcher: The Shooting Script
Erin Brockovich: The Shooting Script
Eternal Sunshine of the Spotless Mind: The Shooting Script
Gods and Monsters: The Shooting Script
Gosford Park: The Shooting Script
Human Nature: The Shooting Script
I ♥ Huckabees: The Shooting Script
The Ice Storm: The Shooting Script
Igby Goes Down: The Shooting Script
Knight's Tale: The Shooting Script
Man on the Moon: The Shooting Script
The Matrix: The Shooting Script
Nurse Betty: The Shooting Script
Pieces of April: The Shooting Script
The People vs. Larry Flynt: The Shooting Script
Punch-Drunk Love: The Shooting Script
Red Dragon: The Shooting Script
The Shawshank Redemption: The Shooting Script
Sideways: The Shooting Script
Snatch: The Shooting Script
Snow Falling on Cedars: The Shooting Script
State and Main: The Shooting Script
Sylvia: The Shooting Script
Traffic: The Shooting Script

OTHER NEWMARKET PICTORIAL MOVIEBOOKS AND NEWMARKET INSIDER FILM BOOKS INCLUDE:

The Age of Innocence: A Portrait of the Film★
Ali: The Movie and The Man★
Amistad: A Celebration of the Film by Steven Spielberg
The Art of The Matrix★
The Art of X2★
Chicago: The Movie and Lyrics★
Cold Mountain: The Journey from Book to Film
Crouching Tiger, Hidden Dragon: A Portrait of the Ang Lee Film★
Dances with Wolves: The Illustrated Story of the Epic Film★
Frida: Bringing Frida Kahlo's Life and Art to Film★
Gladiator: The Making of the Ridley Scott Epic Film
Gods and Generals: The Illustrated Story of the Epic Civil War Film★
In America: A Portrait of the Film★
The Jaws Log
Kinsey: Let's Talk About Sex★
Saving Private Ryan: The Men, The Mission, The Movie
The Sense and Sensibility Screenplay & Diaries★
Vanity Fair: Bringing Thackeray's Timeless Novel to the Screen

★*Includes Screenplay*

CONTENTS

BY PAUL WEITZ

I started out my "career" as a playwright, working the margins of the margins of off-off-Broadway theatre. After a few years of readings and threadbare productions, what I had was a sheaf of the worst reviews *The New York Times* has ever bestowed on a single person. I was working at a theatre bookshop in New York that was slowly going out of business, and whose half-empty shelves were reminiscent of a Soviet grocery store. My father would mail me the occasional check, hoping to avoid the embarrassment of physically handing it to me. It was a fairly grim picture.

I had heard that there was something called a screenplay that required minimal grammatical skills, and that one could write and actually get paid for. I wrote one on my own, and one with my brother. The one I wrote on my own was miserable, and the one I wrote with my brother had some life to it. Enough life that we started getting hired to write more screenplays, an exercise that could not be described as "intellectual," except in the important regard that none of them would ever actually get made.

This lack of prospects for our work did not disappoint me. I was acutely acquainted with the fact that one could easily *not* be paid for one's writing. We worked as "script doctors" on studio comedies, a position more akin to working at Mother Teresa's house of the dying than, say, being an ob/gyn at Cedars-Sinai. Then we were hired to write an interesting script called *Antz*, an animated film starring Woody Allen, who I suspect has still not seen the film.

After *Antz* we got to direct films, and were in the strange position of being able to make the things we wrote. When we finished *About A*

Boy, my brother Chris wanted to do something wildly different. I wanted to write a film of the same scale, a character study overtly set against the backdrop of American cultural issues. If you work in Hollywood, you can't fail to think about ageism and youth obsession. Furthermore I had heard various stories of people being fired or pushed aside at an age when their experience and vitality should make them more desirable. I started to think about how this affects younger people who are in the position of competing with and defeating their potential mentors. So the core relationship of a fifty-one-year-old man with a twenty-six-year-old boss came to mind. And the idea of the twenty-six-year-old falling for the older man's eighteen-year-old daughter seemed to provide enough drama to give the script legs.

Chris was graceful and supportive, I had a great crew, and I had my usual dumb luck with casting. The film ended up being a reasonable approximation of what I had hoped the script could become. Writing the script on my own felt like going back to playwriting. And instead of bumming money off my dad, I was able to bum character traits from him to use for Dennis Quaid's character.

I hope you enjoy the script. Please feel free to shoot your own version.

In Good Company

written by

Paul Weitz

FINAL PRODUCTION DRAFT

A digital alarm clock hits 4:30 AM. The first note of a SONG, the CREDITS MUSIC, starts as a hand turns off the alarm clock.

INT. DAN'S BEDROOM - EARLY MORNING - NIGHT

DAN FOREMAN, age 51, gets out of bed. His wife Ann, 46, mumbles, doesn't open her eyes.

EXT. DAN'S HOUSE - NIGHT

A light goes on in a window.

INT. DAN'S BATHROOM - EARLY MORNING - NIGHT

Dan shaves, showers, it's still dark outside. He looks at the grey in his hair.

INT. DAN'S BEDROOM - EARLY MORNING - NIGHT

Dan gets dressed in the dark. Puts on his tie. Kisses Ann on the forehead. Behind Ann is a picture of Dan's family. Dan tiptoes out.

INT. DAN'S KITCHEN - EARLY MORNING - NIGHT

Dan drinks coffee. On a small TV behind him, a business channel is on. We see anti-WTO riots. Bill Gates. Images of computer chips being manufactured in India. Dan turns the SOUND UP as a new story comes on, the GLOBECOM logo with MERGER RUMORS as a headline.

NEWS ANCHOR

After months of speculation, analysts expect an announcement this week that Globecom International will acquire Waterman Publishing and its flagship magazine, Sports America.

Dan's attention is caught.

NEWS ANCHOR
The man at the helm of Globecom, billionaire media magnate Teddy K, has been on a spending spree recently -- acquiring a food service company, a cable operator, and two telecommunications providers in deals totaling more than 13 billion dollars.
(pause)
And, how did one lucky ferret owner come to own the largest dog-treat manufacturer on the east coast?

Dan turns off the TV. He dumps the used coffee grains in the trash, where he sees the box for...a "Home Pregnancy Test Kit". He lifts it out of the garbage. Glances over at a picture of his daughter Alex in tennis gear on the fridge. Fear washes over his face.

Lights sweep over the window. A car horn BEEPS. Dan looks at his watch.

EXT. DAN'S HOUSE, SUBURBS - EARLY MORNING - NIGHT

Dan gets in a cab.

EXT. AIRPORT - MORNING

A plane takes off.

EXT. KALB AUTOMOTIVE - DAY

Dan gets out of a rental car.

INT. KALB'S OFFICE - DAY

EUGENE KALB is sixty-something, the CEO of Kalb Automotive. He shakes hands with Dan.

KALB
Thanks for the Lakers tickets. The seats were great, and I'm sick of my damn luxury box.

DAN
I hope Taylor had a fun birthday party.

KALB
(smiles)
My grandson had a terrific time. But I still don't want to advertise in the magazine. My son-in-law tells me people don't read anymore. Too much effort moving the eyes back and forth. We're putting our budget into TV, radio and internet.

A pause. We're ready for Dan to launch into a big pitch.

DAN
Okay.

KALB
"Okay?" What does that mean?

DAN
I'm not going to try to sell you.

KALB
Why the hell not? You're a salesman, aren't you?

DAN
Yes. I'm just not a very good one.

KALB
I'll say.

DAN
(laughs)
But I am going to ask you one favor.

Dan takes an issue of SPORTS AMERICA magazine out of his briefcase.

DAN
I'm going to leave you an issue of the magazine. And I'll personally send you a new one every week. I'll call you again in a few weeks, and if you want to, we'll talk. There's a pretty good article comparing today's quarterbacks with Jonny Unitas.

KALB
There's no comparison. Unitas would kick their butts.
(MORE)

KALB (cont'd)
(holds up magazine)
So this is your sales pitch?

DAN
Yeah. I've worked at the magazine for over twenty years, and I believe in it.

KALB
Good for you. You worried about all these rumors that your parent company's gonna be sold?

DAN
Not really. Can't see how it would affect me.

KALB
Well, hopefully it won't.
(gets up)
You know, that Teddy K. character offered to buy my business a few years ago. Wanted to merge us with Pep Boys. I told him to screw himself...who knows, maybe I was dumb. My son-in-law says I'm a dinosaur.

DAN
Hey, don't knock the dinosaurs. They ruled the earth for millions of years. They must have been doing something right.

Kalb laughs. The two of them shake hands.

INT. GLOBECOM CONFERENCE ROOM - DAY

CLOSEUP ON a DINOSAUR, or, more accurately, a cell-phone shaped like a dinosaur, held by CARTER DURYEA, 26, a young executive.

CARTER
We will never be able to reach this significant, untapped market unless we learn to think like them. In point of fact, less than .05 percent of all cell phone users are currently beneath the age of five years old.
(MORE)

CARTER (cont'd)
The Triceratops phone, the T-Rex phone, and the Pterodactyl phone are going to change all that. And...each phone will have its own unique ring.

The cell phone ROARS like a dinosaur.

CARTER
(little kid voice)
Mommy...I want one...buy me one for Christmas...

At the end of the conference table sits STECKLE, the boss of this group of young marketing execs.

STECKLE
P.F.G., Carter. P.F.G.

YOUNG EXEC #1
(whispers to Carter)
What's P.F.G?

CARTER
Pretty frigging good.

Carter makes the phone ROAR again. Steckle looks up from checking the email on his handheld blackberry.

STECKLE
Gentlemen, ladies, I have an announcement to make. It's on. Teddy K. has busted his move, and we are taking over Waterman Publishing.

The room ERUPTS IN APPLAUSE.

STECKLE
The man has vision. He's a maniac. And I guess it's okay for me to tell you, Teddy K has personally asked me to go over there and turn around marketing in the magazine division. So, if you'll excuse me. Carry on.

Steckle gets up and leaves the meeting. Everyone starts talking.

YOUNG EXEC #1
(excited, to Carter)
Waterman Publishing -- wow --

CARTER
Yeah, yeah, yeah --

Carter hurries out the door.

INT. GLOBECOM HALLWAY - DAY

Carter follows Steckle down the hall.

CARTER
Mark! Mark!

He catches up with him, dodging past other people in the hall.

CARTER
Okay, so you're taking me with you. You have to take me with you.

STECKLE
Carter, I'm gonna take that place and whip its fat ass into shape... And...

CARTER
And?

STECKLE
And I want you to come run ad sales at Sports America.

CARTER
I knew it!

STECKLE
The magazine's a cash cow. It's the cornerstone. I mentioned your name to Teddy K. He liked what you did with cell phones.

CARTER
Wait, hold up. Teddy K. knows my _name_?

STECKLE
I'm going to tell you something and I don't want it to go to your head.
(pause)
You're being groomed.

CARTER
I'm being groomed?
(pause)
Mark, thank you. I am going to kick so much ass for you. I will take no prisoners. I will be your ninja assassin!

STECKLE
(cheerful)
Wow, you're the new me!
(beat, dead serious)
No. I'm the new me.
(smiles)
Congratulations!

Steckle walks off. Carter gives a KARATE KICK.

INT. ALEX'S BEDROOM - NIGHT

ALEX, Dan's 18 year old daughter, lies in bed, awake. She has a tennis ball in her hand. She tosses it up in the air, catches it with the same hand, repeating the motion over and over.

EXT. DAN'S HOUSE - NIGHT

A cab pulls up, drops Dan off.

INT. DAN'S KITCHEN - NIGHT

Going through the kitchen. Dan pauses, looks into the wastebasket. The pregnancy kit is gone.

INT. DAN'S HOUSE, CORRIDOR - NIGHT

Dan goes down the hall, opens a door, looks into his 16 year old daughter JANA's room. She's sleeping. He closes the door again. Continues down the hall, takes a deep breath, and looks in on Alex's room.

INT. ALEX'S BEDROOM - NIGHT

ALEX looks up from her bed.

ALEX
Hey, Dad.

DAN
Hey, button. What are you doing awake?

ALEX
(shrugs)
Couldn't sleep.

DAN
Couldn't sleep? Why? You worrying about something?

ALEX
Not really.

DAN
Cause if you are worried about something...you know you can always talk to me. Remember, when you were little, we made a deal, we'd always be honest with each other.

ALEX
(laughs)
Yeah...I actually am a little tired. We're still playing tomorrow, right?

DAN
Sure.

ALEX
Alright, I'll see you then.
(turns off the light)
Love you.

DAN
(stands there a moment)
Love you too.

He closes the door, heading to his bedroom.

INT. DAN'S BEDROOM - NIGHT

Dan's wife ANN, 46, looks up as Dan changes out of his travel clothes.

ANN
What time is it? Hi, sweetheart.

DAN
Little after three. Sorry I woke you up. Go back to sleep.

Dan gets in bed beside her. He kisses her shoulder. She kisses him back.

ANN
You're not tired?

DAN
Not really....Honey, does umm...does Alex have a new boyfriend?

ANN
Uh, no, not that I know of. Why?

DAN
Well...no reason. What about that Myron kid?

ANN
(kisses him)
I think they're just friends.
(pause)
I'm pregnant --

DAN
What?!
(pause)
I'm sorry, I thought you said _you_ were pregnant.
(she nods)
You can't be pregnant.

ANN
I know, but I am.

DAN
But -- How did that happen?

ANN
Well, I think you were there too.

DAN
No, honey. You're done with all that.

ANN
That's what Dr. Steinberg said, but...I guess he was wrong.

DAN
Are you sure?
(she nods)
Holy crap...holy crap! Does it feel like a boy?

ANN
Right now it feels like a stomach flu.

DAN
You can't be serious. Are you serious?
(beat)
Alright...alright. This is going to be fine. When he's twenty-one, I'll be...seventy-two.

ANN
Three.

DAN
Two.

ANN
Three.

DAN
Holy crap.

Dan lays back in bed, staring anxiously up at the ceiling.

INT. CARTER'S HOUSE - NIGHT

CARTER (O.S.)
I am so excited.

Carter is lying in bed with his (newlywed) wife Kimberly. He's on his back. She's facing away from him.

CARTER
I am just so damn excited. Is this excitement contagious, or what?

KIMBERLY
No.

CARTER
I'm being groomed. I am being groomed. Do you understand what that means?

KIMBERLY
That you're a chimpanzee?

CARTER
It means...well, it means we're on the road. It's all falling into place. We can get a bigger house. We can have kids. I mean, we have a life going on here!

KIMBERLY
Carter, it's three AM. How much more enthusiasm are we looking at here? Fifteen minutes? An hour?

CARTER
I don't know, I'm sorry, it's just...Teddy K. knows my name.

KIMBERLY
Are you even qualified for this job?

CARTER
What? Sure. Selling cell phones, selling ad space, it's all the same crap. Anyway, it's just a stepping stone.

EXT. CARTER'S HOUSE - NIGHT

The lone light goes off.

INT. SPORTS AMERICA OFFICE - DAY

CU on computer monitor (spatially same as house) showing news of GlobeCom's takeover of Waterman Publishing. PULL OUT to reveal everyone freaking out in office. MORTY, middle aged, dapper, and morbid, is saying to anyone who will listen (at the moment, THEO, another salesman):

MORTY
We're all going to get fired.

THEO
Anything's possible.

MORTY
It's not possible, it's probable.

LOUIE, barrel chested, frenetic, comes down the hall with ALICIA, a sales woman.

LOUIE
Have you heard about this Teddy K guy?

ALICIA
Everyone's heard of him --

LOUIE
I hear he's an albino, but he covers it up with makeup!

MORTY
Hey, Alicia! Alicia? Are you fired yet?

ALICIA
What? No! Why, are you fired?

INT. DAN'S OFFICE - DAY

A placard on the desk reads DAN FOREMAN -- VP AD SALES. Dan's office has a great view of the city. It's decorated with the memorabilia from Dan's more than twenty years at Sports America.

Dan sits with his boss, ENRIQUE.

DAN
I'm sorry, are you -- are you saying I'm fired?

ENRIQUE
Not yet, not yet, Dan. But I can't predict the future. The thing is, you're not head of ad sales anymore. Carter Duryea is.

DAN
Who the hell is Carter Duryea?

ENRIQUE
Some hotshot from GlobeCom. This is a bummer, Dan. A real bummer. But you're lucky. A lot of people are getting canned immediately, across the company.

DAN
Are you getting fired?

ENRIQUE
Me? No.

DAN
We had our biggest year ever this year. My team works incredibly hard. I'm not going to put up with this.

ENRIQUE
You have to put up with it. I mean, what are you gonna do, start somewhere new? You're not a kid anymore. You know how tough it is out there. Places are cutting back, they're not looking for guys like you who make a decent salary. Hey, I'm as pissed off about this as you are.

DAN
So then why are you smiling?

ENRIQUE
I'm not smiling.

DAN
Your lips are curling up.

ENRIQUE
They do that naturally, Dan.

EXT. MADISON AVE - DAY

Dan's older daughter, Alex, walks into the Waterman Publishing building.

INT. LOBBY, WATERMAN PUBLISHING BUILDING - DAY

Alex gets into an elevator. She's holding a tennis racket. Behind her, Carter HURRIES towards the elevator.

CARTER
Hold up! Please.

Alex uses her racket to hold the door open.

INT. ELEVATOR - DAY

Carter and Alex are alone in the elevator. Alex pushes the button for the 47th floor.

CARTER
47. Going to the Sports America offices?

ALEX
Yup.

CARTER
...What are you, an intern?

ALEX
No. My Dad works there...Are you interning there?

CARTER
I'm starting a new job there.

ALEX
Oh. Cool. Congratulations. That's awesome.

CARTER
Thank you.
(pause)
To be honest, I'm scared shitless. I have no idea what I'm doing.

Alex laughs.

CARTER
Don't tell anyone, okay?

ALEX
(laughs)
Okay. I won't.

She smiles at him. He smiles back. The elevator reaches the floor, the door opens, and Carter's expression turns to one of confidence.

CARTER
After you.

INT. SPORTS AMERICA OFFICE, BY DAN'S OFFICE - DAY

Theo, a salesman, passes by Dan.

THEO
Dan, your daughter's here.

DAN
She is?

Dan starts down the hall.

ALICIA
Hey, Boss, what's this takeover
gonna mean for our stock options?

DAN
I have no idea. And don't call me
"Boss".

INT. SPORTS AMERICA OFFICE, HALLWAY - DAY

From the other direction comes Carter, led by DEBRA, the
receptionist.

DEBRA
(kissing ass)
So nice to meet you, Mr. Colon's
very excited to work with you --

As Dan passes Morty's office, Morty yells to Dan.

MORTY
Dan, you hear anything new? Are we
all fired?

DAN
(distracted)
Can't talk now, Morty --

His head turned towards Morty, DAN WALKS RIGHT INTO CARTER.
It's a real COLLISION. Debra gives a GASP.

CARTER
OOOF!

DAN
Sorry!

CARTER
No, I'm sorry. You alright?

DAN
I'm fine. It was my fault. You
okay?

CARTER
I think so. No broken bones.

DAN
Alright, then. No harm, no foul.

Dan moves on towards the reception area.

INT. RECEPTION, SPORTS AMERICA - DAY

Dan walks up to Alex.

ALEX
Hey, Dad.

DAN
Hey, champ. What are you doing here?

ALEX
Umm, tennis, remember?

DAN
Oh, yeah. Sorry.

ALEX
Is today no good for you?

DAN
(beat)
No, it's fine. Heck with it. Let's go.

EXT. ROOFTOP TENNIS COURT - DAY

Dan and Alex are playing tennis on a rooftop court. Alex SERVES. Dan gets a racket on it, but just barely. The ball goes FLYING.

In fact, she is an awesome tennis player, running Dan ragged around the court. Dan tries to reach a crosscourt shot and tumbles to the ground.

ALEX
You okay?

Dan looks over at his daughter, and does some PUSHUPS.

AFTER their match, they sit on a bench. Dan is drenched.

ALEX
You sort of sucked today.

DAN
I was holding back, to build up your confidence.

ALEX
Yeah right. You're gettin' old.

DAN
Thank you.

ALEX
Dad, remember how I was saying maybe I'd want to transfer to NYU? Well...I got in.

DAN
To NYU? Sweetheart, that's fantastic!
(beat)
But that means...you'd have to live in the city.

ALEX
Yeah...I want to study creative writing, and NYU has a great program.

DAN
How about the tennis team?

ALEX
Dad...I'm not going to be a professional tennis player.

DAN
Well look, button, it's almost as tough being a writer. Living in the city, I don't think it's such a great idea. It can be really lonely, you need street smarts. I just don't think it's a great idea.

ALEX
But I <u>want</u> to try living in the city. I know NYU's a lot more expensive. But it would be such a good experience.

DAN
Yeah. It is more expensive, but...
(pause)
It's your education, that's the most important thing...We can manage it.

She hugs him, elated. Over Alex's shoulder, Dan's face falls, the pressure getting the best of him.

ALEX
(laughs)
Yech, you're like drenched.

When Alex pulls back, he smiles for her sake.

INT. SPORTS AMERICA OFFICE - DAY

Enrique is going down the hall, showing Carter around.

ENRIQUE
This is Morty Wexler. Morty, Carter Duryea.

CARTER
You're on the Ford account, right?

MORTY
Correct.

CARTER
Great to meet you.

MORTY
You too. I'm really looking forward to working with you!

Enrique and Carter move on. Louie comes out of his office.

LOUIE
(in a mincing voice, imitating Morty)
"I'm really *looking forward to working with you."*

Louie makes an "ass-kissing" sound.

MORTY
Bite me.

Further down the hall, Enrique leads Carter towards DAN'S OFFICE.

ENRIQUE
We have a terrific office for you, great view. But it's not cleared out yet.

Enrique takes Carter into DAN'S OFFICE.

ENRIQUE
Not bad, hunh? Excuse me a second, I'm just going to use the little boy's room.

Enrique leaves Carter in Dan's comfortable office. Carter looks at the view.

CARTER
(impressed)
Tasty.

INT. SPORTS AMERICA OFFICE, HALLWAY - DAY

Dan comes back into the office, showered and clean after his game.

INT. DAN'S OFFICE - DAY

Carter is still waiting for Enrique. He is glancing at Dan's FAMILY PHOTOS, as well as photos of Dan with sports stars, etc. when Dan comes in.

DAN
Can I help you?

CARTER
Oh! Sorry, this is your office.

DAN
Yeah.
(beat)
You're the guy I bumped into.

CARTER
Yes. You must be Dan Foreman.
(smiles)
Hi, I'm Carter Duryea.

DAN
<u>You're</u> Carter Duryea?

CARTER
Yes. Great to meet you.

DAN
The Carter Duryea who's coming in
to run ad sales?

CARTER
Correct.

Carter puts his hand out.

DAN
How old are you?

CARTER
Me? I'm twenty-six.

DAN
You're twenty-six...

Dan shakes his hand.

DAN
...and you're my new boss.

CARTER
I guess so...
(wincing)
Hey, that's some...Kung-Fu Grip
you've got there.

Dan lets go of his hand.

DAN
So what kind of experience do you
have in ad sales?

CARTER
Not much.

DAN
How much?

CARTER
None.

DAN
None. Well, that's not much.

CARTER
I'm a fast learner. So now you
know how old _I_ am. How old are
you?

DAN
I'm fifty-one.

CARTER
Wow, that's -- that's crazy.
You're one year older than my
father.

Enrique comes in.

ENRIQUE
Great, you two have met!

CARTER
Yeah, we're good pals already.
(smiles)
Well, nice to meet you.

DAN
Un-hunh. It was a pleasure.

ENRIQUE
Dan, you want this door closed?

DAN
Yeah, why don't you go ahead and
close it.

They exit, Enrique closing the door behind them.

Dan picks up an AUTOGRAPHED BASEBALL.

Across the room is a silver trophy-plate reading "1987
SALESMAN OF THE YEAR".

He takes aim, and WHIPS THE BALL AT THE PLATE, SENDING IT
FLYING.

INT. HALLWAY BY DAN'S OFFICE - DAY

A plate reading DAN FOREMAN, VICE PRESIDENT AD SALES is slid
out of its holder as MOVING MEN transfer Dan's stuff to a
smaller office. Dan steps into his new office, watching the
boxes pile up.

EXT. PORSCHE DEALERSHIP - DAY

Carter walks with a well-dressed man, an uncle, perhaps? The
man looks proud of him.

CARTER
It was pretty unexpected. It's like a pretty big promotion.

PORSCHE DEALER
Wow! That's fantastic! Way to go.

The camera reveals that he is in a Porsche dealership. The man accompanying him is a salesman.

PORSCHE DEALER
(stops in front of a car)
So, the Boxster S-type has more guts. You'll sure feel the extra horsepower. But if you really want to go, I'd say take the Nine Eleven Carrerra.

CARTER
(considers)
I'll take the Nine Eleven.

INT. PORSCHE - DAY

Carter tries out the stereo. The cup holders. The seat warmer.

EXT. PORSCHE DEALERSHIP LOT - LATER

Carter ZOOMS out of the lot in a new, black Porsche Carrerra.

INT. PORSCHE 911 - DAY

CARTER
NICE! TASTY!

Carter is checking himself out in the mirror, distracted, when --

EXT. STREET BY PORSCHE DEALERSHIP - DAY

An SUV SLAMS into the front of his car.

INT. PORSCHE 911 - DAY

The AIRBAG SLAMS Carter back into his seat.

CARTER
Mmmff --

EXT. STREET BY PORSCHE DEALERSHIP - DAY

The Porsche sits there, its front left side CRUMPLED. The SUV driver puts down his cellphone.

SUV DRIVER
I'll call you back.
(calls out)
Jackass!

EXT. CARTER'S HOUSE - NIGHT

The damaged Porsche pulls up into Carter's driveway. Carter gets out, his arm in a sling.

INT. CARTER'S HOUSE - NIGHT

Carter walks in, noticing a couple of SUITCASES by the door.

Kimberly is standing there.

KIMBERLY
Hi.

CARTER
Hi. I uh...I hurt my arm. But I'm okay.

KIMBERLY
I'm glad you're okay. Carter...

She nods to the suitcases.

CARTER
Kim...Kimmy...Again? Come on. Seven months. We've been married seven months. I know things have been a bit off. I've been putting in crazy hours at my job. I know we should have -- we should have gone on a real honeymoon, that was my fault. I should have -- I should have shut off that cell phone -- that thing was ringing off the hook! The good thing is, I can change. This has been a great lesson to me. Thank you.

KIMBERLY
Don't try to sell me, Carter.

CARTER
(plowing on)
Kim, I love you. I want to have children with you.

KIMBERLY
But I don't want to have children with you. I don't even know if I want to have children, period. I told you that. I told you on our second date.

CARTER
I thought you were joking.

KIMBERLY
Carter...is this really such a surprise to you?

CARTER
...Are you...sleeping with someone else?

KIMBERLY
...I was. But I broke up with him.

Carter bursts out laughing.

CARTER
Wow, that must have been rough on him!

She goes and picks up her bags.

KIMBERLY
I'll be at my parents. They're really excited to have me back.

Carter covers his face. We hear a HEARTBEAT.

INT. OBSTETRICIAN'S OFFICE - DAY

Dan stares nervously at Ann as the obstetrician listens for the baby's heartbeat with a "stereo" stethoscope.

OBSTETRICIAN
We're gonna hear two heartbeats now, that strong slower one is yours, mom.

Dan listens as A STRONG, STEADY HEARTBEAT is heard over the scope's amplifier. The obstetrician fishes around.

A QUIETER, FASTER HEARTBEAT is heard beside the bass drum of Ann's pulse.

OBSTETRICIAN
And that...that's your baby's heartbeat.

ANN
Oh my God...

Ann smiles, looking up at Dan, who is looking pale.

OBSTETRICIAN
Nice strong heartbeat. That's your new baby, Dan.

Dan looks stressed out. Subjectively, with Dan, we hear an IRREGULAR beat joining the other beats. He tries to smile, grimacing instead.

ANN
Dan?

DAN
Yes?

ANN
Are you okay?

DAN
Yeah...that's...fantastic...I'm --
I just feel a little -- you know --

CUT TO: Dan's shirt is open, and the doctor is listening to DAN'S HEARTBEAT.

OBSTETRICIAN
Well, you are having a little bit of arrhythmia. Have you been drinking a lot of caffeine? Are you under a lot of stress?

DAN
Well...I did sort of get demoted at work.

OBSTETRICIAN
Ah.

ANN
You what?

DAN
(nods, tries to smile)
We'll talk.

Ann looks shocked.

INT. PORSCHE IN DRIVEWAY - NIGHT

CU McDonalds wrapper on the passenger seat.

Carter sits alone in his Porsche outside his house.

He reclines the car seat as far back as it will go (which isn't far). He curls up to try to sleep in the Porsche.

INT. SPORTS AMERICA CONFERENCE ROOM - DAY

A Grande cup of STARBUCKS coffee is drained by Carter. Carter's assistant, SAMMY, comes up to him holding a new cup.

SAMMY
Another?

CARTER
Yeah, don't even ask, just keep it coming.

Carter starts on the next cappuccino as he goes to the head of a long conference table. The entire sales team, as well as everyone's secretaries, and even a couple of the janitorial staff, are gathered. Dan sits among the rest of the sales team.

CARTER
How was everyone's weekend? Good?
(puts his face in his hand)
I'm sorry, that was...

An uncomfortable pause, as Carter gathers himself.

CARTER
All right! I'd like to thank everyone for joining me. As most of you know, my name's Carter Duryea and I am really excited to be working with such a great group of people.
(MORE)

CARTER (cont'd)
Like Teddy K. says, what makes Globecom great...is the men and women...of Globecom -- is it like a thousand degrees in here, or is it me?
(beat)
It's me.

Morty looks at Dan, concerned.

CARTER
Now I've been given an agenda here, and you're gonna learn this about me, I'm a machine...
(Carter blanks)
What was I saying?

ALICIA
An agenda?

CARTER
Agenda, yes. In order to achieve the goals that have been set out for us, we are going to have to increase ad pages by 20 percent.

There is a MURMUR in the room. Carter sucks down some more coffee.

MORTY
(whispers to Louie)
Shit, I knew it.

DAN
(with disbelief)
Twenty percent? Carter, only a start up magazine can do that.

CARTER
Well I think this team can do it.

MORTY
(tentative)
Uh...How?

DAN
(automatic)
Well, Morty --

CARTER
(cuts him off)
Good question. And the answer...
(an epiphany)
...is synergy.
(MORE)

CARTER (cont'd)
To take it to the next level, we need to team up, we need to synchronize, we need to synergize! We're not alone here. We're not alone! We are now part of one of the biggest multimedia and brand name companies in the universe. Let's take advantage of that. Did you know that one of our sister companies makes Krispity Krunch?

Silence.

DAN
So?

CARTER
So we talk to our brothers and sisters at Krispity Krunch, and we make a deal to supply Sports Factoids for their boxes, so when Joe Couch Potato is snacking, what does he see? Sports America Krispity Krunch Sports Factoids! He's definitely getting more Krispity Krunch, and he's definitely not getting Krunch 'n' Krackle, which looks and tastes exactly the same, but has no sports Factoids. Krispity Krunch is so pleased with the idea that they guarantee twenty-six pages a year. Besides which, they know Teddy K. Is gonna be pissed if they don't pony up. Bingo -- synergy!

DAN
Isn't that cheating?

CARTER
Hell no! And you know what else? We also own Starline Cell Phones. What do we put on their browser?

DAN
Factoids?

CARTER
Yes! Factoids! Synergy! You know what else? Box scores! And ads! We make a deal where one-hundred thousand hits on the internet has an equivalent value of one ad page in our hard copy.
(MORE)

CARTER (cont'd)
Are you getting it, people? The magazine is now just a sort of portal to a synergized world of cross-promotion! Let's open things wide here, people! Let's get psyched!
Come on, let's take the plunge, let's embrace something new!
(pointing)
Louie, are you psyched about this?

LOUIE
...I'm psyched.

CARTER
Okay. Alicia, are you psyched?

ALICIA
Absolutely.

CARTER
You...what's your name?

MAINTENANCE GUY
Hector. I'm in maintenance.

CARTER
Oh. That's cool. Hector, I know you're psyched.

MAINTENANCE GUY
I'M PSYCHED!

CARTER
Alright, Hector's psyched! And if Hector's psyched, then <u>I'm</u> psyched! I am <u>psyched</u> for this team! Who else is psyched!

People call out "I'm psyched!"

MORTY
(leans over to Louie)
Who do you think will be the first to get canned?

LOUIE
(whispers)
My bet's on Dan. He's prehistoric.

INT. JAPANESE RESTAURANT - DAY

Carter and Dan sit at a sushi restaurant. Carter's LEG BOUNCES with nervous energy.

CARTER
I'm glad you could join me for lunch, Dan. Do you like sushi?

DAN
I'll stick with the teriyaki.

CARTER
You should try some! The spicy tuna roll is awesome here. Here, try it!

Carter holds out his plate, which is covered with sushi.

CARTER
Get that. Get that. Go fishin' man.

Dan looks at it a moment, then takes a bite.

DAN
(hates it)
Mmm -- yeah. Really...raw.

CARTER
(talks over him)
So I wanted to talk to you, because the increase in ad pages is only part of the equation in terms of achieving the bottom line my bosses want me to hit. I'm also going to have to get rid of 300 K salary from the sales team, immediately.

DAN
Carter, I don't make that much money.

CARTER
I know what you make, Dan.

DAN
Alright. Well.
(gets up)
I wish you told me I was fired before I ate the goddam fish.

CARTER
Hey, hold on a second, I'm not letting you go here.

DAN
You're not?

CARTER
No. Look, you're an excellent salesman, you ran a good team, and I think there's the potential for you to be an awesome wing man.

DAN
An awesome wing man. Well, Carter, I can see the benefit to you in having an awesome wing man. But what's the benefit to me, at this point in my career, in being an awesome wing man?

CARTER
Well, one benefit, at this point in your career, is you get to keep your job. That's a pretty good benefit, don't you think?

Dan stands there, considering.

INT. SPORTS AMERICA OFFICE - DAY

The salesman are hushed, as SWEARING is heard from down the hall, behind the closed door of Carter's (Dan's old) office.

ENRIQUE (O.S.)
Are you smiling? You're smiling at me -- you think this is funny!

Enrique emerges from Carter's office.

ENRIQUE
That A-HOLE. We'll see how soon this place goes down the SHITTER without me! That LITTLE, SNOT-NOSED BRAT!

Enrique STORMS past where Morty and Dan are drinking coffee. Morty raises his eyebrows at Dan.

MORTY
Maybe there is justice in the world.

Enrique pushes past a group of eavesdropping salespeople on his way to the elevator.

ENRIQUE
You enjoying yourselves? Great.

As Enrique leaves, Alicia and Theo do a little high-five.

INT. CARTER'S (DAN'S OLD) OFFICE - DAY

Having just fired Enrique, Carter sags, leaning his head against the closed door.

MUSIC RISES over the following montage.

INT. DAN'S NEW OFFICE - DAY

Dan puts a copy of the magazine into a Fedex packet to send to EUGENE KALB in Los Angeles.

Sammy, Carter's twenty-something assistant, appears at his door.

SAMMY
(snappy)
Carter's ready for you.

INT. CARTER'S (DAN'S OLD) OFFICE - DAY

The office is empty and stark, absent the clutter of Dan's pictures and memorabilia. Carter hands Dan a booklet of forms in the Globecom blue color.

CARTER
Dan, I'd like you to fill this out, please --

Carter sees Dan glance at the lone photo on his shelf -- a picture of Kimberly. Carter turns the picture over on it's face.

CARTER
It's a 360 evaluation.

DAN
And that is?

CARTER
It's a self-evaluation. They call it 360 because it's supposed to be from every angle. It's corporate policy. It'd be great if you have it on Monday.

Carter pats Dan on the arm, dismissing him.

INT. CONFERENCE ROOM - DAY

Carter addresses a group of buyers, Dan at his side.

CARTER
If you want to get aggressive, if you want to reach that core demographic --

DAN
I believe --

CARTER
(cuts him off)
Not now, Dan.
(to buyers)
Sports America is the top magazine, boys twelve to eighteen, in the country.

Dan deflates a little.

INT. CARTER'S (DAN'S OLD) OFFICE - NIGHT

Late at night. A janitor goes by as Carter works late.

INT. CARTER'S HOUSE - DAY

CLOSEUP PROFILE Carter runs against a jungle background. For a moment it looks as if he's out in the wild. He has a phone to his ear.

KIM'S VOICE (O.S.)
Hi, leave me a message! Or don't.

BEEP.

We PULL BACK, revealing Carter is jogging on a treadmill by his flat-screen TV, which has a nature show on.

CARTER
(leaving message)
Hi, it's me. I mean, you know it's me, I guess I'm...filling up the old mailbox...anyway, call me back. Or don't.

He hangs up. Looks at the phone again.

INT. CARTER'S LIVING ROOM - DAY

Carter squats in front of a fish tank with a single goldfish in it. He TAPS the tank, trying to get the fish's attention.

CARTER
Here boy. Here boy. Here.

INT. CARTER'S HOUSE - DAY

Carter is back on the treadmill, calling an old friend.

CARTER
Oh, hi, Mrs. Charneski, is Jeff there? Oh, he did? Okay, well, please tell him Carter said hi.

INT. DAN'S HOUSE, SUBURBS

Dan sits watching TV. The PHONE RINGS.

DAN
Hello?

INT. CARTER'S LIVING ROOM - DAY

Carter waves at the goldfish.

CARTER
Here boy. HEY.

The fish is oblivious.

INT. DAN'S HOUSE - NIGHT

Dan sits eating popcorn, watching TV. The phone rings.

CARTER (O.S.)
Hey, Dan! Carter here.

DAN
Who?

CARTER (O.S.)
(chuckles)
Carter Duryea. Listen, I'd like to get the group together tomorrow and go over some business development ideas.

DAN
Tomorrow's Sunday.

CARTER (O.S.)
Right! We'd get a great jump on the week. I'm not talking the whole day, just the afternoon, meet at noon, I'll order some sushi, it'll be fun. Great!

Carter hangs up. Dan looks at the phone, shocked.

EXT. MADISON AVE - DAY

Dan walks up to the building on Sunday, looking angry.

INT. SPORTS AMERICA OFFICE - DAY

Dan walks into the Sports America office. It's empty.

INT. CARTER'S (DAN'S OLD) OFFICE - DAY

Carter sits at his desk, pressing his fingers into his eyes.

STECKLE (O.S.)
What the hell are you doing?

From Carter's POV, we see Steckle in double.

CARTER
Uh, nothing, just...seeing stars. You ever do that?

STECKLE
Yeah, when I was three.

CARTER
What are you doing here on a Sunday?

STECKLE
Sunday is a fun day to kick some ass.

CARTER
Absolutely. Hey, my team's coming in. Dan Foreman's here, you should meet him.

STECKLE
Yeah, I'd rather not get personally involved. Didn't we decide to let him go?

CARTER
No, I let go of Enrique Colon instead, remember?

STECKLE
Oh, yeah, that's right. Did a little "Colon Cleansing". Get it?

CARTER
(laughs)
That's good. Hey, you want to have dinner tonight?

STECKLE
Wish I could, but I'm flying to Berlin to meet with some of our satellite guys.

CARTER
(disappointed)
Oh. That's too bad.

STECKLE
Why? Something wrong?

CARTER
No, just...
(beat)
Ah, my wife and I are having a few problems...

STECKLE
Okay, gotta go. Look, you're gonna have to riff some more people.

CARTER
Riff them?

STECKLE
Reduction in forces. Shitcan them.

CARTER
Listen, I -- I think we can get pages up, so we don't have to riff anyone yet.

STECKLE
Fine. But sooner or later, we all have to deal with reality.

Steckle leaves.

INT. HALL BY CONFERENCE ROOM - NIGHT

Night. A group of salesmen are leaving the imposed Sunday meeting. Carter stands outside the door, still full of energy, saying goodbye as everyone finally leaves to go home.

CARTER
Great work, thanks for coming in! Night, Morty! Night Louie! What are you guys up to? Want to go out for a beer?

LOUIE
I'd love to, but I'm a recovering alcoholic.

CARTER
Oh. Better not then. Morty?

MORTY
I'd better get home for dinner. My wife is slowly poisoning me to death, and she gets very angry if I'm late.

CARTER
(beat)
Okay. No problemo. Alicia?

ALICIA
No, I have to get home and do my hair.

CARTER
Hey, Dan, want to grab a beer?

DAN
I have to go have dinner with my
family.
(joking)
You want to have dinner with my
family?

CARTER
(quickly)
Sure! That would be great! Thanks
a lot! Just let me get my stuff
together.

DAN
Hey, wait --

But Carter is already off. Dan is surprised and annoyed that Carter is taking him up on his mock offer.

EXT. DAN'S HOUSE, SUBURBS - NIGHT

Carter's unwashed, dented Porsche pulls up to the house. Carter has a lead foot on the brakes.

DAN
Who taught you how to drive?

CARTER
Uh, no one.

DAN
No kidding.

INT. DAN'S HOUSE, LIVING ROOM - NIGHT

Ann comes out from the kitchen as Dan and Carter come in.

CARTER
Now this is a house! I mean, like
a home-type house, you know what I
mean?

DAN
Yes. Sweetheart, this is Carter
Duryea from the office.

ANN
(fake smile)
Oh. Hello. Nice to meet you.

CARTER
Hi, Mrs. Foreman. Thanks so much for having me in your home.

Carter HUGS Ann, who is taken by surprise.

ANN
Uhh -- You're very welcome. I hope you like baked ziti.

CARTER
I love baked ziti. Baked ziti. Exactly! That is exactly what I need. Fantastic. Home cooking. Awesome.

INT. DAN'S HOUSE, KITCHEN - NIGHT

Ann and Dan are in the kitchen.

ANN
Is there something wrong with him?

DAN
Clearly. Let's just feed him and get him the hell out of here.

ANN
He really is young. At least, a lot younger than you.

DAN
Thanks for that.

ANN
I did the numbers on NYU today. Do you know how expensive that school is? Plus living expenses. Plus Jana's orthodonture. Plus baby costs.

DAN
Hey, don't worry about it.

ANN
That's not actually a solution to a problem: "Don't worry about it." I think we might have to take out a second mortgage.

DAN
Maybe I should go into the living room and ask my boss for a raise.

INT. DAN'S HOUSE, LIVING ROOM - NIGHT

Carter is looking at framed family photos on the mantle. He stares at the happy photographs, his expression is as if he's trying to decipher runes.

Alex comes down the stairs, followed by Jana.

Alex stops short.

CARTER
Oh, hi! I was just looking at you in these photographs, and you were, you've -- I never actually introduced myself in the elevator. I'm Carter Duryea --

ALEX
I know who you are. Does my Dad know you're here?

CARTER
Your Dad invited me for dinner. Technically.

JANA
Who's this?

ALEX
This is Dad's new boss.

JANA
You can't be Dad's new boss. You're too young.

ALEX
He's also "scared shitless".

CARTER
Hey. Good memory.

JANA
Plus you're too cute to be Dad's boss.

CARTER
Really? Thanks.

The PHONE RINGS.

JANA
(yells)
I'VE GOT IT!

She RUNS UPSTAIRS to answer, leaving Alex and Carter alone.

CARTER
So, how's it going?

Alex looks at him like he's weird.

ALEX
I'm okay. What are you doing here, really?

CARTER
Really? My wife left me, and today's the anniversary of our first date, and I found the idea of going home to my house to be too depressing, so I sort of leeched onto your Dad and invited myself over.

ALEX
...You're sort of a bizarrely honest guy, hunh?

CARTER
Not really. Just with you, for some reason. Most people would probably say I'm an anal-retentive, emotionally guarded asshole.

The two of them stand there a moment.

ALEX
(pause)
You want to play foosball?

CARTER
Okay.

ALEX
Okay. Just let me...change.

INT. DAN'S HOUSE, KITCHEN - NIGHT

Ann is opening the oven.

DAN
You think Alex can cope with living in New York on her own?

ANN
I'm less worried about her coping with it than I am about you.

DAN
Yeah, frankly I'd rather keep her under house arrest with a homing device on her ankle.

ANN
So then why'd you agree to it without even talking to me? And why is your teenage boss here? And why do I feel so nauseous -- I hardly had any morning sickness the first two times! I'm sick of it!

DAN
Alright, alright, calm down...let me get that --

Dan GRABS THE HOT CASSEROLE DISH with his BARE HANDS --

DAN
OWW! SHIT!

He DROPS THE CASSEROLE, SHATTERING IT on the floor, splashing tomato sauce on his pants.

Ann just looks at him. Then she leans over to be sick in the sink.

INT. DAN'S HOUSE, GARAGE - NIGHT

Alex is kicking Carter's ass at FOOSBALL.

ALEX
I'm just not that into tennis anymore, and what I'm really not into is being "the tennis jock," you know? It's like people don't even invite me to parties because they think I'm in training. Also there's this rumor going around that I'm a lesbian.

CARTER
That sucks. I mean -- not being a lesbian, but --

ALEX
Well, I'm not.
(she smashes the ball)
It would be one thing if I was going to go pro and make a ton of money, but I'm not at that level. I've played girls who are that level, and I'm not. Not that I'd want to be, really. Their lives have peaked by the time they're like twenty-one.

Carter retrieves the ball.

CARTER
Sometimes I wonder if my life has peaked at 26. If it's all downhill from here.

ALEX
It probably is.

CARTER
Yeah, probably.

INT. DAN'S HOUSE, LIVING ROOM - NIGHT

Dan is at the door, paying a pizza delivery guy.

DAN
Thanks. Keep the change.

He closes the door with his foot.

DAN
(calls upstairs)
DINNER'S READY.

JANA
(from upstairs)
I'M ON AN IMPORTANT CALL.

DAN
WITH WHO?

JANA
MY BOYFRIEND.

DAN
Your what?

Dan puts down the pizzas, picks up the phone.

DAN
Hi, this is Mr. Foreman. Who is this, and how old are you?
(pause)
Alright, Will, I just wanted to say that if you ever give my daughter an alcoholic beverage or a joint, I will hunt you down and neuter you.

JANA
DAD!!!

Dan hangs up.

DAN
DINNER'S READY.

INT. DAN'S HOUSE, GARAGE - NIGHT

Dan comes into the rec room. Sees Carter and Alex RALLYING.

DAN
There you are. You kids ready to come inside for dinner?

Dan pauses, realizing he's just called his boss a "kid" to his face.

Alex and Carter look at each other.

INT. DAN'S DINING ROOM - NIGHT

A family tableau. Everyone talking and eating at the same time.

CARTER
Mmm. Great pizza. Where'd you get it?

ANN
It's from a wonderful little Italian restaurant called Dominoes.

JANA
So are you really Dad's boss?

CARTER
(swallows, glances at Dan)
We're more -- colleagues.

DAN
(takes another slice)
That's not true. He's the boss
man. I'm the wing man.

JANA
Are you married? You're wearing a
wedding ring.

CARTER
Yeah. Sort of. Yes. Yes.

JANA
So you're like...prematurely old.

ANN
Jana, would you pass the pizza?

CARTER
I've got it.

Carter REACHES FOR THE PIZZA at the same time as Jana, KNOCKING OVER A SODA. It SPILLS ONTO DAN'S LAP.

DAN
DAMMIT!

CARTER
Sorry!

DAN
That's okay. Never mind.

CARTER
Let me --

Carter tries to WIPE DAN'S LAP with his napkin.

DAN
Carter, only my wife is allowed to
touch me there. Now excuse me. I
have to change my pants. Again.

Dan leaves the dining room. Carter smiles sheepishly.

ALEX
(to Carter)
Good job.

CARTER
Thanks.

INT. DAN'S HOUSE - NIGHT

Carter is leaving the house, waving goodbye. Dan and Ann are in the doorway.

CARTER
Bye, thank you so much, that was a great dinner! Terrific pepperoni.

ANN
You're very welcome.

DAN
Goodbye. Go home.

Dan shuts the door.

EXT. DAN'S HOUSE, SUBURBS - NIGHT

CARTER
(to the shut door)
Thanks again.

Carter turns, goes back to his car.

Behind him, ALEX IS WATCHING HIM from the window. He glances back over his shoulder, and she DUCKS BEHIND THE DRAPE.

INT. DAN'S HOUSE - NIGHT

Alex looks a little puzzled with herself. She looks again, as...

EXT. DAN'S HOUSE - NIGHT

Carter pulls out jerkily from the house.

INT. CARTER'S HOUSE - NIGHT

Carter stands in his empty living room. He tips a table lamp gently, balancing it until it falls off the table.

EXT. NYU DORM HIGH-RISE - DAY

Alex moves into her dorm. Dan unloads her stuff out of his station wagon.

EXT. TRIBECA APARTMENT BUILDING - DAY

A couple of movers help Carter move into his new apartment.

INT. ALEX'S DORM - DAY

Dan carries a box past a POSTER OF A CANNABIS LEAF on another student's door. He frowns.

EXT. NYU DORM HIGH-RISE - DAY

Alex walks Dan out to his car. The two of them HUG.

DAN
Here's some pepper spray.

Dan hands her some pepper spray on a chain.

ALEX
Thanks, that's sweet.

DAN
Oh, and I've installed surveillance devices throughout the dorm so I can tell if you're doing anything bad.

ALEX
Okay.

DAN
Okay. Be careful.

Dan turns his face away, hiding his emotion, and quickly gets into his car.

EXT. BANK - DAY

Ann and Dan walk into a bank MORTGAGE LOAN office.

INT. BANK - DAY

Dan and Ann are in the BANK LOAN OFFICE, filling out forms for a second mortgage.

LOAN OFFICER
Sign here, here, and here, and you've got your second mortgage.

Dan looks at Ann. She smiles at him, a bit ruefully.

Dan SIGNS.

INT. DIVORCE LAWYER'S OFFICE - DAY

Carter SIGNS papers.

Carter is sitting in a LAWYER'S OFFICE, filling out forms for his divorce.

DIVORCE LAWYER
Sign there, there...and there. And it's official...

Carter FINISHES SIGNING.

DIVORCE LAWYER
You're divorced.

INT. DAN'S NEW OFFICE - DAY

Carter is in Dan's office.

CARTER
Alright, two things. First, Steckle wants to organize a company basketball league. I'm captain of the sales team. You're power forward. Second, I heard you're taking the Rums of Jamaica guys to a Knicks game on Wednesday night. You should have run that by me.

DAN
Run it by you? They're my clients.

CARTER
No, they're GlobeCom clients. So we're taking them to the Globecom luxury suite.

DAN
These aren't luxury suite kind of guys.

CARTER
Dan, everyone is a luxury suite kind of guy. The suite's being used on Wednesday -- Teddy K's hosting Bill Clinton, Jay-Z and Kofi Annan -- so we'll take them to a concert on Thursday.

DAN
A concert?

CARTER
The thing is, we need to get them to up their buy for this year by eighteen pages. We have to start kicking some ass here, or I have to let some people go.

DAN
Why do you say "let them go?" They don't want to go. Why don't you just say "fire them?"

CARTER
Because it sounds better.

DAN
Not to the person getting fired it doesn't.

Carter looks at Dan.

EXT. MADISON SQUARE GARDEN - NIGHT

The lights on the marquee read TONIGHT: LEGALLY DEDD.

INT. LUXURY SUITE - NIGHT

A well-stocked corporate luxury suite, high above the concert floor. Dan, Carter, Morty, Louie, and a couple of other sales people shmooze their guests from Rums of Jamaica as HARDCORE HIP-HOP PLAYS BENEATH THEM. A waitress in hip-hop gear serves drinks.

CORWIN, mid-fifties, black, from Philadelphia, not Jamaica, is the head ad buyer for Rums of Jamaica.

CARTER
Apparently, he was shot twelve times, and pronounced "legally dead", hence the name.

CORWIN
Someone should tell him it's spelled D-e-a-d.

DAN
They're afraid to.

CARTER
He has a number one song out right now. He's a protege of Fifty Cent.

DAN
Why don't they call him "Nickel?"

CARTER
What?

CORWIN
(laughs)
In twenty years, your jokes haven't improved.

CARTER
Anyone want another rum and coke? Corwin?

CORWIN
Nope, I'm okay. But I am glad it's all Jamaican rum.

CARTER
Oh, this is Petey from K-JAM sneakers.

PETEY
I'm excited to talk to you about the possibility of a cross-promotion where if you buy a certain amount of Jamaican rum, you get a discount on running shoes.

CORWIN
Un-hunh...sounds like a great fit. Get a lot of drunk people running around. Hey, Dan, you want to go get some air?

DAN
Sure. I'll be back in a bit,
Carter.

CARTER
No problem. But don't be too long,
we got chimichangas on the way!

EXT. MADISON SQUARE GARDEN SEATS - NIGHT

Dan and Corwin walk on the street outside MSG.

DAN
Sorry about this concert. They
wouldn't let me just get normal
seats for the Knicks game.

CORWIN
That's okay. Dan, I've been
instructed not to advertise in
Sports America any more.

DAN
(shocked)
What?

CORWIN
We were bought out last year by a
company called Continental Brands.
Apparently, the company that bought
us and the company that bought you
guys are having a feud over
wireless communications in Europe.

DAN
Wireless communications? What the
hell does that have to do with our
business?

CORWIN
Nothing. But we have this
corporate policy now. I just found
out about it, or I wouldn't have
yanked your chain by coming here
tonight.
(sighs)
I'm sorry, Dan.

INT. BAR NEAR MSG - NIGHT

Dan and Carter sit in a bar. Carter drinks beer. Dan drinks scotch on the rocks.

DAN
We'll get those ad pages back. We'll just have to work a little harder to fill 'em.

CARTER
You don't get it. Steckle gave me a bottom line. We had to increase pages this quarter.

The drink.

CARTER
...Dan, I have to...I have to fire Louie and Morty.

DAN
No you don't.

CARTER
Yeah, I do. We've got Alicia, Pete, and Harry on the Ford account. So Morty is a logical choice. And the new woman at Pepsi thinks Louie's a sexist, guess why? He called her sugartits.

DAN
That idiot. Look, you can't fire those guys. These are my guys. They've been with me for eight years -- I hired them at the same time.

CARTER
I know. That's why they have big, bloated salaries, that are not commensurate with what they bring in. I'm sorry.

DAN
(pause)
I've been here twenty-three years. My salary's higher than theirs. Why don't you just fire me?

CARTER
(angry)
You want me to fire you Dan?
Because I could.
(heated)
You have a family that loves you.
You have a new kid on the way. I
look at you sometimes, and it's
like...
(pause)
You have people who need you. You
really want to put them in jeopardy
for Morty and Louie?

Dan looks at him.

INT. DAN'S HOUSE, SUBURBS - NIGHT

Dan comes up the stairs, the alcohol apparent in his plodding walk.

Dan looks in at Jana's room.

His younger daughter sleeps peacefully.

INT. DAN'S BEDROOM - NIGHT

Late at night. Dan sits on his bed.

Ann reaches up and touches him on the shoulder.

Then he gets in beside Ann.

She pulls him closer. He puts his hand on her belly. Ann closes her eyes. Dan's eyes stay open.

INT. CARTER'S (DAN'S OLD) OFFICE - MORNING

Carter is sleeping on his couch. Dan comes into the office.

DAN
What are you, living here now?

CARTER
What? What time is it?

DAN
Seven AM. Look, I've been thinking
all night.
(MORE)

DAN (cont'd)
And...if it has to be done...I should be the one to do it.

INT. DAN'S NEW OFFICE - DAY

Morty and Louie sit on Dan's couch as Dan closes the blinds.

DAN
Guys, I feel...really terrible about what I'm about to say, but...I'm afraid you're both being...let go.

LOUIE
Being let go? What does that mean?

DAN
It means...you're fired. Believe me, if I had any choice in the matter...I just thought you should hear it from me, because I'm the one who hired you.

LOUIE
Wait a minute, are you getting fired too?

DAN
...No. This...this isn't my decision.

LOUIE
Oh, so...it's not your decision so you're not to blame.

DAN
I didn't say that.

LOUIE
I can't believe this. You were -- you were like a brother to me. I would have stepped in front of a bus for you, you piece of shit. You know, you've become a real corporate asshole.

DAN
Louie --

LOUIE
I tell you what, if you see my friend Dan, tell him I was looking for him.

DAN
Louie!

Louie leaves. Dan looks shocked.

MORTY
Dan...what the hell am I going to tell my wife? I mean...she already wears the pants. Now she's gonna wear the tie and jacket too.

DAN
Morty...I'm sorry.

Morty starts to cry.

MORTY
I know this must have been hard for you. You were a good boss, Dan. I mean it. You always treated everyone with respect. And...well I appreciate it.

They shake hands. Dan avoids his eyes.

Morty leaves, Dan stands at the interior window. Tries to open the blinds. Can't bring himself to.

INT. CARTER'S (DAN'S OLD) OFFICE - DAY

Carter is sitting on an exercise bike, peddling. Dan comes in, hands Carter something.

CARTER
What's this?

DAN
My 360 self-evaluation.

CARTER
...You've rated yourself "Does not meet expectations."

DAN
Yeah.

Dan turns and leaves.

INT. SPORTS AMERICA OFFICE - DAY

Morty leaves the office, carrying a bedraggled houseplant.

Colleagues shake his hand, hug him goodbye.

EXT. SOHO STREET - DAY

Carter walks down the street in Soho, checking out stores.

He sees Alex sitting at a cafe alone.

EXT. SOHO CAFE - DAY

Carter comes over to Alex.

CARTER
Hey! What are you doing here?

ALEX
Oh, hey! Nothing, just reading.
I'm going to NYU now.

CARTER
Awesome, you did it.

ALEX
How about you?

CARTER
I rented an apartment. In Tribeca.

ALEX
That's awesome.
(pause)
Do you drink coffee?

CARTER
No, usually I just hook up to an
IV.

EXT. CAFE TABLE - DAY (LATER)

TWO EMPTY ESPRESSO CUPS sit next to the FULL ONE Carter is nursing.

Carter is sitting with Alex at the cafe table, his leg bouncing nervously.

ALEX
You sure can pound back the
caffeine. Is that why your leg is
shaking like that?

CARTER
I think it is.

ALEX
Your wedding ring's gone.

CARTER
Uh, yeah. I am officially the first guy from my high-school class to get a divorce.

ALEX
Oh. Sorry.

CARTER
That's okay. If I look at it honestly, it's been coming since... pretty much our second date. So umm...how's school?

ALEX
Pretty good!
(pause, less upbeat)
Pretty good. I mean, it's sort of hard to get to know people, coming in as a transfer. Everybody has already joined their clique and they're not sure if they can admit one more. My creative writing classes are cool, though.

CARTER
Creative writing, hunh?

ALEX
Yeah, I guess I've always been interested in stories. Escaping into someone else's life. Because mine seemed pretty boring. I'm cursed with a functional family. Of course writing isn't exactly practical, so I'm thinking of getting a double major in business.

CARTER
Oh, man, don't do that. Stick with writing.

ALEX
You know, sometimes you seem sort of bummed out with your career or something, which is weird because you're so successful.

CARTER
No, I'm not bummed out. It's pretty much what I have in life, you know, my career. That and a dented Porsche.

ALEX
Well your family must be really proud of you.

CARTER
(shrugs)
My mom is, maybe, I don't know. She was sort of a hippy, so she's not so into the corporate stuff. And my dad left home when I was four, so...I don't know the guy. His parents had money, but he was this "artist", in quotes, he was kind of a druggy, he was in this cult for a while-- hey, let's get out of here, you want to maybe...go for a walk or something? Now that you know my entire life story?

ALEX
Sure, but there's not much left to talk about.

She smiles at him. He smiles, enjoying being kidded.

CARTER
...Right.

EXT. SOHO STREET - DAY

Alex and Carter walk down the street, talking nonstop.

EXT. STREET, CHINATOWN - DAY

Alex and Carter walk down the street in Chinatown, past a fish market. They try to avoid the fish guts on the pavement. Carter is making Alex laugh.

EXT. STREET, LITTLE ITALY - NIGHT

Alex and Carter come out of an Italian restaurant in Little Italy.

Alex kisses him, stopping him in his tracks.

CARTER
Right.

Carter looks a little stunned.

ALEX
Umm, you want to see my dorm room,
maybe?

Carter laughs nervously.

ALEX
Look, don't get the wrong idea,
it's not like I uh...have guys up
to my dorm room often. Or ever,
actually...

Carter takes a breath.

CARTER
...Okay.

ALEX
Okay.

INT. DORM HALL - NIGHT

Alex leads Carter down the hall towards her room. Music
blares out from various rooms as they go past.

CARTER
I am having a major college
flashback.

ALEX
Come on, old man.
(opens a door)
My roommate's out tonight.

CARTER
Oh. I was...really looking forward
to meeting her.

ALEX
Yeah, she's...only mildly
chemically imbalanced.

INT. ALEX'S DORM ROOM - NIGHT

A college dorm room, half of which is Alex's, half of which is decorated primarily in black.

ALEX
Ta-daa!

CARTER
Wow. This is awesome.

ALEX
Yeah, it's okay.

Alex takes off her scarf by a "GLOBECOM" banner which has been graffitied to read 'GLOBECOM SUCKS."

ALEX
Umm...so...

CARTER
So...yeah...I heard this...this rumor that alcohol impairs your judgement --

She starts UNBUTTONING CARTER'S SHIRT.

CARTER
Hold on -- wait --

ALEX
(stops)
Yes?

CARTER
Umm...I wish you weren't so beautiful.

ALEX
I'm not.

CARTER
Actually, you are.

ALEX
Thank you.

Attempting to set the mood, Alex light some incense -- Puts on some music -- Turns on a lamp, drapes a tie-dyed shirt over it -- MELLOW LIGHT fills the room.

CARTER
(gently)
Well I...I think everything's perfect now...

ALEX
Then why are you still talking?

They kiss. Alex starts to laugh.

CARTER
What?

ALEX
I was just thinking how my dad said he put surveillance devices all over the building.

CARTER
Uh, yeah...that's very funny...

He glances up at the ceiling as she PULLS HIM ONTO THE BED.

CUT TO:

INT. SPORTS AMERICA OFFICE - DAY

Dan WATCHING SOMETHING. Widen out -- He is drinking coffee, watching as around him there is PANDEMONIUM. Moving men are all over, packing up people's offices.

DAN
(to moving man)
Where to now?

MOVING MAN #1
You're all going to the 29th floor.

DAN
I hear there's great air-conditioning on that floor.

INT. HALL BY DAN'S OFFICE - DAY

Carter comes down the hall, sees Dan, and halts for a second in fear (he has just slept with Dan's daughter), then waves to him, overcompensating.

CARTER
(almost shouts)
Hi, Dan! How was your commute?
(MORE)

CARTER (cont'd)
Boy, can you believe they're moving our offices again? Hey, our first hoops league game is gonna be against the 51st floor, corporate VP's -- which is now apparently gonna be this floor!

DAN
What's wrong with you?

CARTER
What? Me? Nothing. Why?

DAN
You're acting jumpy. You switch from Mocha to crack?

CARTER
You are really, really, paranoid, you know that?! Crack. Ha-ha!

Carter turns a corner, flattens himself against the wall, and EXHALES.

MUSIC RISES.

EXT. NYU DORM HIGH-RISE - NIGHT

Carter picks Alex up for a date in his Porsche.

The Porsche has finally been fixed.

Alex steps out of the dorm to meet him in a LONG, SEXY DRESS.

Carter looks smitten.

INT. TENNIS BUBBLE - DAY

Carter and Alex play tennis. Alex is drinking a soda while hitting with Carter.

CARTER
You know, that's completely demoralizing.

Alex laughs.

ALEX
Sorry.

INT. ALEX'S ROOM - DAY

Ann and Dan are constructing a crib in Alex's room. Dan is getting frustrated, trying to jam a spindle into a socket.

ANN
Don't force it. Don't force it.

Dan forces it, and the bottom of the crib FALLS with a CRASH.

DAN
(looks at her)
Don't say it.

INT. DAN'S HOUSE, KITCHEN - NIGHT

Ann writes CHECKS for various BILLS, while in the background, Dan leaves a message for Alex.

DAN
Hi there, Alex, haven't talked to you in a few days, give us a call.
(hangs up, presses redial)
...Okay, guess you have your cellphone off. Give us a call.
(to Ann)
Should I try again?

ANN
Yeah, maybe the first twenty times were a fluke.

INT. EXPENSIVE RESTAURANT - DAY

Carter slaps down a CREDIT CARD for a fancy lunch with Alex.

INT. TARGET - DAY

Dan puts down his credit card, buying a cart full of BULK ITEMS at Target with Ann.

INT. CARTER'S 2ND NEW OFFICE - DAY

Carter closes his blinds.

Carter fires a member of the sales team.

SALESMAN
(stunned)
...I'm fired?

CARTER
I'm sorry.

Then another.

SALESWOMAN
But I've worked here for five
years?

Carter reaches over and grabs some tissues, and hands them to...

Sammy, his eager assistant.

Sammy, who has been fired as well, is crying. He blows his nose and shakes Carter's hand.

SAMMY
It's been an honor.

Carter pats Sammy on the back.

INT. SPORTS AMERICA HALLWAY - DAY

Chairs and desks pile up in the hall, as moving men break down the empty office spaces caused by layoffs.

INT. CARTER'S OFFICE - DAY

Carter runs in place by his desk.

INT. HALLWAY 29TH FLOOR - DAY

Alicia pauses, seeing Carter running in place through his window.

INT. CARTER'S 2ND NEW OFFICE - DAY

Carter looks over, realizes he's being watched.

EXT. WATERMAN PUBLISHING (NOW GLOBECOM) BUILDING - DAY

Snow falls outside the building.

EXT. CENTRAL PARK - DAY

Snow blankets the city.

INT. GYMNASIUM - NIGHT

BALLS BOUNCING. Night. AN INDOOR BASKETBALL COURT. First game of the company league.

The Sports America ad sales team is in gray jerseys with SALES RATS on them. The corporate VP team, which includes Steckle, is in slick GLOBECOM TROTTERS jerseys.

Dan is sliding a bulky knee brace over his leg.

CARTER
Jeez, you gonna be okay?

DAN
I'll be fine. What's that guy doing here? He's one of the moving men.

Dan nods to a 6'6" guy who's on Steckle's team. The moving man DUNKS.

CARTER
I guess Steckle recruited him for the corporate VP team.

DAN
Well that's fair.
(looks up at basket)
Wonder if I can still dunk.

CARTER
You could dunk?

DAN
Yeah. Can't you? You're only 26.

STECKLE (O.S.)
Heads up!

Carter FLINCHES as Steckle pretends to whip a ball at him. Carter chuckles.

STECKLE
(to Carter)
Word on the street is that Teddy K's on the prowl.
(MORE)

STECKLE (cont'd)
Soon as he gets back from his 'round the world balloon trip he's gonna go munch on Continental Brands.

DAN
Great. Maybe they'll advertise in our magazines again.

Carter flinches as Steckle focuses on Dan like a shark.

STECKLE
I'm sorry, who are you?

CARTER
Mark, this is Dan Foreman. Dan just closed the Toys R Us deal.

DAN
Carter's being modest, he did most of the work.

STECKLE
That's beautiful, maybe you two should get a room.

Dan's face gets red.

STECKLE
You pussies ready to be schooled?

Carter tries to laugh it off as Steckle dribbles away. Dan looks pissed.

THE GAME STARTS.

Steckle and Dan match up.

The 6'6" moving man is a ringer. But so's Dan. The moving man dominates inside, while Dan knocks down outside shots. Steckle gets more and more pissed, as Dan takes him to school. The big man starts to double-team Dan.

Dan BANGS down underneath the basket, GRABBING A REBOUND, and is REJECTED by the big moving man. The VP TEAM CHEERS.

STECKLE
(in Dan's face)
YEEAAAH! Not in my house!

A look of annoyance at Steckle crosses Carter's face.

At the other end, Steckle passes to the big man. Dan goes to double team him, and he passes back to Steckle who hits an EASY LAYUP.

STECKLE
Sweetness! You can't guard me!

Dan swallows his anger.

Next trip upcourt, Dan gets double teamed. He makes a neat pass to Carter, who makes an open layup.

CARTER
Yes!

Carter and Dan share a moment, pointing at each other across the court.

DAN
(to Theo)
I'll take big man.

Next trip down the court, Dan guards the big guy. He is UP IN HIS JOCKSTRAP, keeping within a foot of him at all times.

6'6" MOVING MAN
Hey, ease up old man, don't have a heart attack.

DAN
What's the matter, big man, can't take a little D?

Dan KNOCKS a pass away from him. At the other end, Dan gets the ball back on a pass, starts to SHOOT when Steckle BLOCKS/FOULS him.

STECKLE
RE-JEC-TION!

Dan glares at Steckle.

The VP team runs upcourt. Steckle STREAKS DOWN THE COURT, going up for an EASY LAYUP, when Dan RUNS UP from out of nowhere, BLOCKING THE SHOT.

DAN
Not in my house.

Dan sprints down to the other end, catching a pass and going for THE DUNK.

Dan's team cheers.

CARTER
Dunk it!

DAN SKIES...ALMOST MAKING IT...

BUT THE BALL CATCHES THE RIM INSTEAD, causing Dan to LOSE HIS BALANCE.

Dan COMES DOWN AWKWARDLY, SLAMMING into the court.

Dan hops up quickly, his shoulder GROTESQUELY out of joint.

CARTER
Oh, shit.

Everyone looks a little disgusted.

Steckle stifles a laugh.

EXT. DAN'S 2ND OFFICE WINDOW - DAY

We see Dan's smaller new office from OUTSIDE the building.

Dan is making a phone call. He comes up to the window, his arm in a sling.

On the other end of the line is Alex's answering machine.

ALEX (O.S.)
Hi, you've reached Alex's cell.
Please leave a message.

Dan hangs up the phone.

We dolly over to see CARTER standing at the window in his adjoining office. Carter is staring at the city, musing.

Carter turns and sits down at his desk.

INT. CARTER'S 2ND NEW OFFICE - DAY

Carter's screen saver is the GlobeCom logo. He hits a button, and a picture of ALEX fills the screen.

Carter sits looking at the photo, an intimate closeup.

DAN (O.S.)
So what's her name?

Carter hits a button and gets rid of the picture of Alex. Dan is at the door - he hasn't seen it.

CARTER
(freaked)
What? Who?

DAN
The fish.

CARTER
Oh. It's uh...it's a he, and his
name's Buddy.

DAN
Doesn't he want a friend?

CARTER
He had a friend, but...he ate him.
How's your shoulder?

DAN
Keeps popping out. You mind?
(Carter nods)
Tell me something, when you were
eighteen, did you ever return your
parents' phone calls?

CARTER
Uh, well, they never called, but I
guess I would have.

DAN
My older daughter won't call me
back. I feel like going to NYU and
kidnapping her, so I can stop
worrying about her.

CARTER
Well, that, that sounds like a not
great idea. Anyway, Alex seems --
from the very brief time I met her -
- to be pretty savvy.
(in a reverie)
I wouldn't worry about her too
much. She's a terrific, smart
woman. Girl. Young lady.
whatever. My point is, she can
handle herself.
(pause)
You seem to have a really great
marriage...How do you do it?

DAN
You just pick the right one to be
in the foxhole with. And then...
(MORE)

DAN (cont'd)
when you're outside of the foxhole, you keep your dick in your pants.

CARTER
Wow, that's...poetic.

Dan nods. Carter smiles.

INT. DAN'S HOUSE, LIVING ROOM - DAY

A FOOTBALL-SHAPED CAKE with HAPPY FIFTY-SECOND BIRTHDAY written on it is placed on the table by Ann.

Ann's pregnancy is very visible now.

A SURPRISE PARTY is in the works. The living room is full.

We see people from work -- Alicia, Theo, etc. among the crowd.

Carter comes in.

CARTER
Hey, Theo, how's it --

Theo mumbles hello as he blows past Carter.

Carter finds himself standing by a preteen kid holding a wrapped basketball.

CARTER
(with present)
Hey, where do I put this?

The kid points to a gifts table.

Carter stands around a moment, trying to bond.

CARTER
This party's a rager, hunh?

The kid nods unenthusiastically.

CARTER
Okay.

Carter heads over to the gifts table.

EXT. DAN'S HOUSE, SUBURBS - DAY

Dan's Volvo station wagon drives towards the house.

INT. DAN'S STATION WAGON - DAY

Dan drives towards the house with Jana.

JANA
Are you still glad you decided not
to have a birthday party?

DAN
Yup. I'm not in the mood this
year.

JANA
Well, Mom says you could use a
little fun. She says you should
lighten up for the sake of your
health.

DAN
She does, does she?

Looking towards his house, Dan sees a little MOVEMENT behind
one of the drapes.

INT. DAN'S HOUSE, LIVING ROOM - DAY

Alex pulls away from peeking out the window.

ALEX
They're here! Everybody hide!

EXT. DAN'S HOUSE - DAY

Dan and Jana get out of the car. Dan pauses, looking towards
the house.

DAN
You go ahead, I just want to put an
envelope in the mailbox.

Dan watches Jana go ahead into the house. Then he TAKES OFF
HIS COAT.

INT. LIVING ROOM - DAY

Jana comes in, excited.

JANA
Quiet -- he's coming in in a minute! Everyone hide!

Everyone hides.

EXT. DAN'S HOUSE - DAY

Dan is now TAKING OFF HIS SHIRT. He KICKS OFF HIS SHOES.

INT. DAN'S HOUSE, LIVING ROOM - DAY

We hear the FRONT DOOR OPEN. Everyone leaps up and YELLS:

EVERYONE
SURPRISE!!!

We see everyone's face register SHOCK. Ann DROPS THE CAMERA she was holding.

REVERSE from their POV

Dan is standing at the door in his UNDERPANTS, SMILING.

DAN
Wow! What a surprise!

Dan MOONS the partygoers. Everypne SHRIEKS.

JANA
(horrified)
DAAAD!!!

INT. DAN'S HOUSE, KITCHEN - DAY

LATER. Dan, fully clothed now, drinks punch, chatting with some friends, when Morty comes over.

DAN
Morty! Good to see you! Thanks for coming. How are you?

MORTY
Not so good. Not so good. I mean, psychologically.

DAN
Oh. I'm sorry.

MORTY
That's okay. Anyway, my wife got a promotion. I'm hoping she'll raise my allowance.
(pats Dan on shoulder)
But this is good punch.

Morty walks off.

INT. CARTER'S PORSCHE, DRIVEWAY - DAY

Carter and Alex sit in Carter's Porsche.

ALEX
I better get back inside, they're going to notice I'm missing.

CARTER
Yeah, I just wanted to give you a gift.

Carter hands her a box.

ALEX
It's not my birthday.

She opens it. It's a pendant with small diamonds in it.

ALEX
Holy shit, are these real diamonds?

CARTER
No, they're cubic zyrkonium. Yeah, they're real.

ALEX
These are too much, I can't take them.

CARTER
No, I'm sorry --

ALEX
I feel funny, I --

CARTER
No, don't feel --

ALEX
It's sweet. Very sweet.

CARTER
Oh. Good, thanks.

They kiss. Then they both quickly look over at the house where the party is going on.

CARTER
Alex, I've really been thinking, and...you're the kind of person who's good to be in a foxhole with.

ALEX
But we're not in a foxhole. We're in a Porsche.

INT. LIVING ROOM - DAY

The party is in swing. Dan is unwrapping presents -- mostly shoulder braces, boxes of Ben Gay, etc, as people cheer. Dan looks out the window.

EXT. DAN'S HOUSE, SUBURBS - DAY

Carter and Alex walk back to the party, holding hands for a moment.

INT. LIVING ROOM - DAY

Dan sees Carter and Alex holding hands. Then they break apart as they approach the house.

Dan looks like he's had the wind knocked out of him. Did he just see what he thought he saw?

INT. NEW SPORTS AMERICA OFFICES, ELEVATORS - DAY

The elevator door opens, Carter steps in, and Dan stops the elevator.

DAN
Hey, I thought maybe we could have lunch today. Go over some stuff.

CARTER
I'd love to, but I already have a lunch.

DAN
Oh yeah? With who?

CARTER
(beat)
With Wally Hebert from Proctor and Gamble.

DAN
Don't you want your wing man along?

CARTER
Uh, not today.

The elevator closes, leaving Dan there. The other elevator opens, some people step out. A beat. Dan steps in.

EXT. MADISON AVE - DAY

Carter hails a cab. From the building lobby, Dan is WATCHING HIM.

Dan hails a cab too.

EXT. DOWNTOWN STREET - DAY

Carter goes inside a trendy restaurant.

INT. DOWNTOWN RESTAURANT - DAY

Carter joins Alex at a table.

CARTER
Sorry I'm late. It's really been a hell of a day.

ALEX
That's okay. But I have a three o'clock class.

EXT. DOWNTOWN STREET - DAY

Dan is on the street outside the restaurant. Trying to stay hidden, Dan looks through the restaurant window. He FREEZES as he sees CARTER AND ALEX sitting inside.

INT. CHELSEA RESTAURANT - DAY

Carter and Alex's waiter comes over.

CARTER
Hey, you're wearing the necklace!

ALEX
Yeah.
(makes a face)
I feel like an imposter. I mean, it's great, but --

CARTER
An imposter? You look beautiful, doesn't she look beautiful?

WAITER
She does -- now we have three specials today. Avocado soup with Awapuhi oil. Calamari fritti with awapuhi. We have bluefin tuna with jalapeno, drizzled with awapuhi. We also have poached Maine lobster -

CARTER
May I get a side of awapuhi oil with that, please?

Alex laughs.

INT. FRONT OF RESTAURANT - DAY

Dan walks by the maitre d'.

MAITRE D'
(smiles)
Welcome, may I help you?

Dan walks right past.

At the table, the waiter is still reading the specials.

CARTER
(looking up)
Holy shit.

ALEX
(freaked)
Dad?!

Dan stands there, glowering.

WAITER
Hi, is there going to be a third?

DAN
I have just one question. Are you sleeping with him?

WAITER
I'm gonna go get you folks some bread.

The waiter retreats.

CARTER
Dan, this isn't what it looks like.

DAN
Oh, really? What does it look like? Tell me. WHAT DO YOU THINK IT LOOKS LIKE?

CARTER
Well...it probably looks like some kind of...tawdry, sleazy affair, kind of thing, but --

DAN
Alex, I asked you a question. Are you sleeping with him?

ALEX
What do you want me to say, Dad?

Alex looks down at her plate.

DAN
(to Carter)
Get up.

CARTER
What?

DAN
Get up.

A beat. Carter gets up.

Dan PUNCHES HIM IN THE EYE, sending Carter FLYING BACKWARDS OVER HIS CHAIR.

People in the restaurant GASP.

Dan WINCES, holding his hurt shoulder.

ALEX
Dad! Stop! It's not his fault!

The maitre d' comes over.

MAITRE D'
Sir, I don't think you ahould --

DAN
(wheels on him)
You'd better back off before I drop kick you across this restaurant.

The maitre d' veers away.

Carter is on the floor.

CARTER
Oww -- Jesus.

DAN
(to Carter)
You are a piece of shit.

CARTER
Dan, I love her.

DAN
You what?

CARTER
I love her.
(to Alex)
I love you.

Alex hides her face.

DAN
You love her? She's my daughter!

CARTER
I know...

DAN
She's in college. She's a college student. I took out a frigging second mortgage so she could go there! Three years ago I was paying orthodonture bills for her!

Alex starts to cry.

CARTER
I'm sorry.

DAN
(to Alex)
This guy? You had to sleep with him?

Dan turns and walks out of the restaurant. Alex gets up.

EXT. RESTAURANT - DAY

Dan leaves the restaurant, followed by Alex.

ALEX
Dad! Dad! Wait! I'm sorry, it's not -- this had nothing to do with you!

DAN
He's my boss, Alex!

ALEX
That's not...I wasn't thinking of that. It just happened.

DAN
We made a deal, remember? We made a deal to always be honest with each other.

ALEX
Dad, I was five years old when we made that deal.

DAN
Yeah. I liked you better then.

ALEX
That's an awful -- an awful thing to say -- wait, don't walk away from me, let's talk -- let's talk about this --

DAN
Why? You clearly don't need my advice about anything.

Dan walks off, leaving Alex crying.

MUSIC RISES.

EXT. CENTRAL PARK - DAY

Dan sits down on a bench. Takes off his tie. He looks shattered.

EXT. DOWNTOWN STREET - DAY

Carter walks towards NYU, his eye blossoming purple.

INT. ALEX'S DORM ROOM - DAY

Carter comes in. Alex and her roommate are there.

ALEX'S ROOMMATE
Hey, Carter, wow, that's some shiner.

ALEX
Could we have some privacy, Maya?

ALEX'S ROOMMATE
Sure. Absolutely.

The roommate leaves.

ALEX
Have a seat. You want some ice for that?

CARTER
Yes, please.

Alex goes to a mini-fridge.

ALEX
Umm, we don't have any ice left. But here, this soda's cold.

She hands Carter a cold soda, which he puts on his eye.

CARTER
So, umm...sorry about my timing there, with uh...the L word. It just sort of slipped out. But I've been thinking about it a lot, and that's how I feel.

ALEX
Umm -- that's really sweet.

CARTER
I mean it.

ALEX
I know you probably think you do.
But I've been thinking too, and I'm
-- I'm doing a double major.

CARTER
(nodding)
Yeah...

ALEX
And I'm taking anthropology classes
on top of that. I've got a lot
going on.

CARTER
Yeah...absolutely...

ALEX
I'm not really ready for a big
commitment.

Carter tries to play it off like something positive.

CARTER
Yes. Absolutely. That's what I'm
talking about. Look, when I said I
loved you I didn't mean that I
wanted to...interfere with your
classes, I mean...I'm not talking
about marriage or anything. Yet.

ALEX
Carter, I've had a great time, and
I think you're a really great guy,
but...You're on the rebound.

CARTER
I'm not.

ALEX
It wasn't all that long ago that
your wife left you.

CARTER
That was the best thing that ever
happened to me.

ALEX
Well...good. But then it's a good thing whether you're with me or not. And I...I think we should stop seeing each other.

Carter assumes the same cajoling expression he had when Kim left him.

CARTER
Alex. Aleeex...

Alex looks Carter in the eyes. She looks open, vulnerable. The look freezes Carter. He drops the sell job he had been trying to do.

CARTER
I just want to tell you...
(beat)
I've enjoyed talking to you more than pretty much anyone in my entire life.

ALEX
(swallows)
Thank you...Me too.

Carter nods.

Turns and leaves Alex's dorm room. The sound of the door opening transitions us to...

INT. DAN'S HOUSE, LIVING ROOM - NIGHT

Dan comes into the living room, looking exhausted.

Jana comes down from the top of the stairs.

JANA
Dad?! Where have you been? Your cell phone was off.

DAN
Why? What is it?
(beat)
Where's mom?

EXT. SUBURBAN HOSPITAL - NIGHT

Dan and Jana park Dan's Volvo.

Dan RUNS out, ahead of Jana, SLAMMING the car door behind him.

INT. ANN'S HOSPITAL ROOM - NIGHT

Dan comes in, finds Ann lying peacefully in a hospital bed.

ANN
There you are.

DAN
You okay?

ANN
I'm fine. The baby's fine. I had a little scare. There was some bleeding.

DAN
What was it?

ANN
A uterine tear. It sounds bad, but it's okay. I just need some rest.

Dan controls himself.

DAN
Sorry. I'm just glad you're okay.

He wipes his eyes.

DAN
I just...I don't know what the hell I would do if anything ever happened to you. I think I would pack it in.

ANN
Well, I'm afraid you're gonna be stuck with me for a while.

She kisses his hand.

For the first time that day, Dan becomes calm.

INT. ANN'S HOSPITAL ROOM - LATER

Late at night. Dan sits by Ann's bed as she sleeps.

The door opens, and Alex comes in.

She looks at her mom.

ALEX
Is she okay?

DAN
(whispers)
Yeah. Sleeping.

He puts his finger over his lips. Gets up.

INT. HOSPITAL CORRIDOR - NIGHT

Dan and Alex sit in a small waiting area. Dan has a paper cup of coffee.

ALEX
I broke up with Carter.

DAN
Why? Because of me?

ALEX
No. Because of me. Anyway, I'm sorry.

DAN
For what?

ALEX
Lying to you. Hiding stuff from you.

Dan picks at the lid of the coffee cup.

ALEX
I should tell you, Carter didn't seduce me. If anything, it was the other way around.

DAN
Please, I don't need the details --
(beat)
Unless, I mean, you want to tell me.

ALEX
Uh, no. Not particularly.

DAN
Good.

ALEX
You probably think I'm disgusting.

DAN
Disgusting? Why on earth would I
think that?

ALEX
..I didn't know you took out a
second mortgage. I don't have to
go to NYU. SUNY's fine.

DAN
No --

ALEX
Its fine.

DAN
(firm)
No. You're staying at NYU...

Dan gathers himself.

DAN
Look, Alex, you're a...a smart
woman. You can handle yourself.
And what I'm saying is...I'm going
to try, okay? To...be whatever
kind of father I should now be for
you. I'm not saying I can pull it
off, but...I'm gonna try and...
adjust.

ALEX
(touched)
Dad...you don't have to change.

DAN
Yeah...I do.

Dan pats her on the shoulder.

EXT. MADISON AVENUE - DAY

High angle shot on the city. Taxis, buses, people going by
from skyscraper perspective.

INT. ASSISTANTS' DESKS - DAY

Three computer screens pop to "TEDDY K. IS COMING", one after the other.

A saleswoman reacts with surprise as Teddy K's jovial face pops onto her screen.

INT. CONFERENCE ROOM - DAY

Moving men lift out the table.

They set up the room. Plug stuff in. Set up a podium.

Steckle appears. Greets some of Teddy K's staff. More and more people fill the space.

INT. HUGE CONFERENCE ROOM - DAY

About a HUNDRED-FIFTY PEOPLE are JAMMED into the room, including Theo, Alicia and the remaining sales staff.

TEDDY K emerges from the elevator bank, with his beautiful, somewhat robotic assistant at his side. It's hard to tell how old he is. He could be a mature-looking 40, or a young-looking 60.

The crowd parts before him, staring, amazed, at the great man.

Teddy is naturally charming, working the room.

TEDDY K.
Hi! How are ya! Good to see ya!
(to secretary)
Nice brooch!
(joking to assistant)
We must be paying her too much money!

Teddy moves into the conference room, SHAKING PEOPLE'S HANDS, GIVING HIGH-FIVES.

TEDDY K.
(greeting people)
Hi, hi, how are you, hi.

Teddy's assistant whispers in his ear as he approaches Steckle.

TEDDY K'S ASSISTANT
(in Teddy's ear)
Mark Steckle.

TEDDY K.
(smiles at Steckle)
Mark Steckle! How are ya?!

Steckle beams.

STECKLE
Hi, Teddy!

TEDDY K.
How ya doin?

STECKLE
Very psyched!

Steckle leads him through the crowd, stopping by Carter.

STECKLE
Oh, this is Carter Duryea.

TEDDY K.
Oh, yes, cell phones.

CARTER
Thanks! I'm with Sports America
now.

TEDDY K.
That's the flagship.
(pauses)
What happened to your eye?

STECKLE
Yeah, what did happen?

All eyes are on Carter.

CARTER
Oh, I...fell asleep at my computer.
(mimes it)
Bang. Right on the monitor.

TEDDY K.
Well...those things can be
dangerous!

Teddy laughs, which is the cue for everyone else to laugh!

TEDDY K.
Well keep up the good work! Keep in touch!

Teddy K. gives Carter the thumbs up sign, and moves on.

STECKLE
(whispers to Carter)
I wouldn't be surprised if he announces another takeover today.

Teddy stands at a podium. He looks out at the crowd, as everyone settles in their seats.

TEDDY K.
Synergy.

The room lights go down. Teddy is bathed in the blue glow from a rear-projected Globecom logo behind him.

Carter looks over to see Dan, who comes out of the elevator. He is in yesterday's clothes, having spent the night at the hospital.

TEDDY K.
What exactly does it mean? Why does a business swim with it, and sink without it, in this new ocean of megabytes, streaming video, and satellites?

Dan makes his way into the crowd.

TEDDY K.
There are vast differences between us. On a person to person level, on a national level, on a global level. Every day, the world becomes more complex.

The crowd gazes at Teddy, mesmerized.

TEDDY K.
And to survive in a complex world, we need complex bonds to interface with it.

The audience hangs on his words. Dan watches him with narrowed eyes.

TEDDY K.
What we're building here. Is it a company, or is it an economy?
(MORE)

TEDDY K. (cont'd)
Is it a new country, with no national boundaries, a new democracy of the consumer? A new democracy with a new electorate. Twenty-four hour music videos in Kuala Lumpur. Computers with parts manufactured in Japan, Greenland, Idaho and India. A soft-drink ad going out simultaneously to seven continents? The Dalai Llama eating Krispity Krunch while uploading prayers onto the net?
(pauses)
In this room. In this room, I see this.

Teddy K. Holds up his hands, FINGERS EXTENDED. Wiggles them.

TEDDY K.
What we're trying to get to is this.

Teddy K. INTERLACES HIS FINGERS, mimicking the GLOBECOM CORPORATE LOGO.

TEDDY K.
(smiles)
This is unbreakable. This is inevitable. Woman's World magazine. Why not a Woman's World channel? Across the world. Computers. Why not a weekly computers section in Sports America magazine?

Someone in the audience LAUGHS.

It's Dan.

All heads turn towards him.

He looks a little surprised at himself.

DAN
Uh, excuse me. Excuse me.

TEDDY K.
(puzzled)
Yes?

There is murmuring in crowd.

DAN
I'm sorry. My uh...My name's Dan Foreman. I...I work for Sports America...and...I'm not sure I understand what you're talking about.

Carter looks at Dan, shocked.

Dan proceeds, tentatively.

DAN
What I mean is, what do computers have to do with sports? Are you literally saying there should be a section in the magazine about computers? Who's going to want to read that?

Steckle shoots Dan a look of DEEP HATRED.

DAN
And I'm not sure I understand how the way the world is changing is actually going to change how we do business. I mean, we still are selling a product which someone hopefully needs, right? We're still just human beings, with other human beings as customers.

Dan picks up steam.

DAN
And I can't see how this company is like its own country. I mean, just because we sell all different kinds of things, that doesn't mean we should operate by our own laws, does it? Besides which, countries, at least democratic ones, have some obligations to their citizens, don't they? So how do layoffs and bottom-line thinking fit into that?

There is a long pause.

TEDDY K.
...Dan Foreman.

Teddy nods gravely.

TEDDY K.
...Sports America...you ask some excellent questions.
(nods)
Some excellent, excellent questions.
(mulling it over)
I'm glad you asked them.
(pause)
And I'm leaving it to you...
(gazes at the crowd sternly)
...to <u>all</u> of you, to answer them.
And now, unfortunately...
(to his assistant)
Absolutely.

Teddy K. LEAVES THE ROOM, followed by his assistant.

There is a pause. Everyone is silent.

Then Steckle starts APPLAUDING TEDDY K.

STECKLE
YEAH! TEDDY K!

Everyone else in the room JOINS HIM in applauding.

STECKLE
TEDDY K!!!

Dan walks out through the back of the crowd, who are all facing away from him, towards the departing Teddy K.

INT. DAN'S OFFICE - DAY

Dan sits behind his desk. Carter comes in.

CARTER
Oh my God. Oh my God, Dan.

Steckle comes in.

STECKLE
Good, you're both in here.
(points at Carter)
You I'll deal with in a second.
(to Dan)
You. Have you lost your frigging mind?

DAN
Well, he...he said they were excellent questions.

CARTER
Dan --

STECKLE
Okay, you think this is funny. You think it's funny to disrespect a great man. Do you know who you were talking to just now? Teddy K! TEDDY K, GODAMMIT!
(pause)
Look, we've been carrying your fat, bloated salary for way too long. I want you out of this building within the next ten minutes. Now I'm gonna go to my office and smoke a nice cuban cigar, and try to forget you ever existed.
(to Carter)
In my office. Now.

Steckle turns to go.

CARTER
Mark...Don't fire him.

STECKLE
Excuse me?

CARTER
He busts his ass, Mark...and...

STECKLE
(aggressive)
And?

CARTER
Nothing.

Dan looks down, embarrassed and defeated.

CARTER
Just...if you fire him...
(pause)
You have to fire me too.

Dan looks at Carter, surprised.

STECKLE
...I'm sorry. Let me get something straight. You're throwing yourself in with <u>him</u>? With this useless, over the hill loser? Think here, think what you're doing, because if you're not careful, you're gonna end up like him.

CARTER
I guess...I guess...that would be okay.

STECKLE
(beat)
Alright. Then you're fired too, you little shit.

CARTER
...That's too bad, because...you're going to lose a huge client Dan and I were working on. It was going to save the year for us. Without it, magazine's pretty deep in the red.

STECKLE
Oh yeah? What client is that?

Pause. Carter glances at Dan. Dan looks at Steckle.

DAN
...You think we're going to tell you?

Steckle stares at Dan.

STECKLE
...You're bluffing.

DAN
I don't bluff...I'm not that good a salesman.

STECKLE
(beat)
Okay, well I don't give a crap.

CARTER
I think Teddy K. will. See, I'm gonna call him, and tell him you drove his most profitable magazine, his flagship, into the ground. And he'll listen to me.
(MORE)

CARTER (cont'd)
(beat)
He likes what I did with cell phones.

Steckle looks from Carter to Dan. It's a standoff.

STECKLE
You have 24 hours. Or you're both gone.

Steckle leaves.

CARTER
(beat)
Any ideas?

Dan thinks...

DAN
...One.

EXT. PARKING LOT, KALB AUTOMOTIVE - DAY

Los Angeles.

Dan and Carter get out of their rental car.

Carter looks nervous. Dan smiles at him reassuringly.

EXT. BRIDGE, CORPORATE CAMPUS - DAY

Dan and Carter walk towards the Kalb Automotive building.

DAN
You got all your research?
(Carter nods)
Alright. Follow my lead.

He pats Carter on the arm.

INT. LARGE OFFICE - DAY

Dan hands a copy of SPORTS AMERICA to Morton Kalb.

DAN
Thought I'd bring you this in person again.

KALB
Thanks. How are your daughters?

DAN
They're great, thanks. And your grandkids?

KALB
They're fine. My son-in-law has my oldest, Ralphie, enrolled in a computer camp, whatever that is.

Carter approaches, laughing a little too loud. Kalb looks at him as if noticing him for the first time.

DAN
I'd like to introduce my boss, Carter Duryea.

KALB
Your boss? He looks more like your nephew.

CARTER
Well I've...been learning a lot from Dan.

KALB
What happened to your eye?

DAN
That's one of the things he's learned from me.

An uncomfortable pause. Carter tries to laugh this off.

KALB
Are you saying you punched him in the eye? Why?

CARTER
We don't really have to get into this.

KALB
Please, I'm...rather curious.

DAN
(to Carter)
Why _did_ I hit you?

Carter gives Dan a look. What the hell is Dan thinking?

DAN
(pauses, then shrugs)
...He called me a dinosaur.
(MORE)

DAN (cont'd)
Said I was out of date, and I'd better step in line.

Dan looks at Carter. Carter's eyes widen a touch.

Kalb looks surprised.

KALB
So you slugged him?

DAN
It was a fair fight.
(to Carter)
Right?

Carter picks up the ball.

CARTER
Right.
(taking out a folder)
Mr. Kalb, you have a truly impressive business. I've been looking into all the details, new franchise openings, market awareness, customer demographics --

KALB
I'm sorry, you got into a fistfight because he called you a dinosaur?

DAN
I don't know what happened. I just snapped. There's only so much a man can put up with.

KALB
Hunh. And...if you're his boss, why didn't you fire him?

CARTER
(pause)
He's my best salesman. Now I've been looking at a cross-promotion we could do with Krispity-Krunch --

DAN
(cuts him off)
Carter, that's okay. Mr. Kalb, I don't want to go into facts and figures right now. You know them all anyway. Let me just ask you, what's your hesitation about advertising in the magazine?

Kalb watches the two of them.

KALB
...My hesitation is that our advertising budget is already overextended. My son-in-law spent a lot of money on cable and on-line, and, frankly, we're not getting the bang for the buck that we hoped for. He wants to plow more money into it, but...

DAN
...But?

Kalb looks from Carter to Dan.

KALB
But he is such an asshole.

Kalb's anger spills out.

KALB
I built this business, and I know more about running it than he ever will. And I know that when I make a mistake, it doesn't pay to retrench. I'm going to restructure our whole advertising plan. Starting with a major buy in your magazine.

DAN
That's great news, Mr. Kalb! Thank you.

CARTER
Thank you so much!

Dan and Kalb shake hands.

KALB
(to Carter)
Oh, and...I don't give a shit about Krispity Krunch. Let's just stick to the magazine.

Kalb walks Dan towards the door.

KALB
(to Dan)
So you really slugged him?

DAN
Yup.
(snaps his fingers)
Carter.

Carter follows him out.

EXT. BRIDGE, CORPORATE CAMPUS - DAY

Dan and Carter arrive at the office.

CARTER
That was awesome! You were amazing! I mean, that was actually...fun!

DAN
(laughs)
What Kalb really needed was to see an old fart who beat the crap out of a kid half his age. And you know what the best thing is? It's the right thing for him to do. It's gonna improve his business.

CARTER
(stops)
...You actually...you actually believe in this stuff, don't you?

DAN
(stops)
Course I do. Why the hell else would I do it?

Dan walks off down the bridge, doing a little dance.

INT. SPORTS AMERICA OFFICE - DAY

Dan and Carter get off the elevator, still on a high. Alicia sees them.

ALICIA
Dan, where have you been?!

DAN
We were in Los Angeles.

CARTER
We made a huge sale.

ALICIA
Congratulations. So did Teddy K.
He sold the company! To Calcor
Communications!

CARTER
What? That can't be!

Carter and Dan stand there, speechless.

INT. STECKLE'S OFFICE - DAY

Carter and Dan come in.

CARTER
Mark! What happened? I thought
you said Teddy K was going to buy
another company!

STECKLE
That's what they told me, but -- he
sold us...I'm out.

CARTER
Wait, _you're_ out?

STECKLE
Yeah. They're reorganizing the
whole place.
(to Carter)
You're out too.

Carter looks stunned.

STECKLE
(to Dan)
I think you're in.

DAN
I'm in what?

STECKLE
Your old job.

DAN
My old job? Running the
department?

STECKLE
That's the rumor.

(MORE)

STECKLE (cont'd)
(he sits back, shattered)
The whole thing seems so arbitrary.
I feel used.

DAN
(pause)
Yeah. Kinda tough to know you're
replaceable, hunh?

He looks at both of them.

DAN
I'm sorry you lost your jobs.

MUSIC RISES.

EXT. TRIBECA APARTMENT - NIGHT

Carter sits on the street outside his apartment.

He thinks.

INT. DAN'S FIRST OFFICE - DAY

Dan stands in his old office. The walls are empty.

He has boxes of his stuff piled in the middle of the room.

EXT. STREET - DAY

Carter walks towards the camera in his business suit.

INTERCUT WITH

INT. DAN'S FIRST OFFICE - DAY

Dan puts all his old memorabilia, pictures, etc. back up on
the shelves and walls, taking posession of his office again.

EXT. STREET - DAY

Carter walks closer to the camera as the music CRESCENDOES.

INT. SPORTS AMERICA OFFICE - DAY

The elevator BINGS, and Carter steps through the doors into
the office.

He is dressed in sweats and jeans, looking like a kid for the first time in the movie.

He walks down the hall, looking around, looking a little lost.

INT. DAN'S OFFICE - DAY

Dan is back in his old office. He stands as Carter comes in.

CARTER
Hi, Dan.

DAN
Carter. Come on in.

CARTER
Nice office.

DAN
Thanks. Have a seat.

Carter sits.

DAN
So. How have you been the last month?

CARTER
I've been good, thanks. It's been...pretty strange not having to get up and go into work in the morning.

DAN
Yeah. Well that's what I wanted to talk to you about.
(pause)
I want to offer you a job. We definitely...had our moments. But I think you're a good manager, and a good salesman, and I'd like you to come here and be my second in command.

CARTER
(surprised)
Dan...I really appreciate that, more than you know. And if I knew this was what I wanted to do, there's no one I could learn more from than you.
(MORE)

CARTER (cont'd)
But I'm not sure what I want to do for a living. I'm not sure I want to work at a big place. I thought I did. I thought I had everything mapped out. But...I'm not really sure what I want to do with my life. I just know I want it to mean something to me, like this means something to you.

DAN
Oh.

CARTER
Do you think I'm being stupid?

DAN
(pause)
...No, I don't. I think that sounds right.

Carter nods.

He settles back.

CARTER
So how's...the family?

DAN
Ann's good. Baby's coming Tuesday after next Tuesday. Caesarian.

CARTER
Wow. That's amazing.

DAN
It sure is.
(pause)
And the girls...the girls are both good.

CARTER
I'm glad. Please...give them all my best.

Pause. Carter gets up.

DAN
So what are you going to do?

CARTER
I've saved up a bit of money, I'm going to travel.

DAN
That'll be fun.

Carter stands there for a moment.

CARTER
Umm...Dan...thanks.

DAN
...For what?

CARTER
For...I guess for showing me a few things. No one ever took the time to umm...give me a hard time before. Or to teach me anything...actually worth learning. See, I never really had a...

Carter takes a breath.

He scowls a bit, FIGHTING BACK THE EMOTION which has snuck up on him.

Dan looks down.

CARTER
...Sorry. You know what I'm saying.

DAN
Yeah. I do.

CARTER
...Alright.

DAN
Listen, Carter. I want to tell you something. You're gonna be okay.

CARTER
You think so?

DAN
Yeah. I know it. You're a good man.

Carter stands there. It's the first time he's ever heard this.

Carter goes over to Dan and HUGS him.

Dan awkwardly pats Carter on the back. Then he HUGS Carter.

They release the hug. Carter rubs his eye.

DAN
Don't be a stranger.

They shake hands.

INT. LOBBY - DAY

Carter steps out if the elevator and sees Morty waiting to get on among a group of office workers.

CARTER
Hey, Morty! You're back!

MORTY
Yeah! Back in the saddle! Look at you, you're -- you look like a delivery guy.
(turns)
Hey, do you know Dan's daughter Alex?

As some people move through Carter sees Alex approaching. She's carrying her tennis gear.

CARTER
(shocked)
Oh -- hi, yeah -- what are you -- what are you doing here?

ALEX
(shocked)
Oh -- I'm just...surprising my dad, seeing if he wants to play tennis...

MORTY
(oblivious)
Alex is a fantastic tennis player. She was a junior champ, right?

CARTER
Oh, really, you...you play tennis, hunh?

ALEX
(smiles)
...Yeah. So, umm...how's it going?

CARTER
Good, I'm actually uh...leaving town. Think I might try and teach, or...open an awapuhi store. I don't know. You...doing good?

ALEX
Yeah, I'm...just...working on some short stories...

CARTER
That's...that's great.

Morty looks from one to the other.

MORTY
Well, I got a raise! Dan got me a raise, which is a good thing, because my wife just got laid off. Timing's everything in life, right?

Another elevator door opens. People get in.

MORTY (CONT'D)
(getting in elevator)
Take care, Carter!

CARTER
Yeah, you too, Morty. Nice to...nice to see both of you again.

ALEX
Yeah, it was really good to see you, Carter.

Alex gets in the elevator. As the doors close, she lifts her hand in a goodbye to Carter.

Carter turns and walks away from the elevator.

EXT. SUBURBAN HOSPITAL - DAY

And PUSH IN towards the hospital.

INT. HOSPITAL MATERNITY WARD, WAITING ROOM - DAY

Alex and Jana are sitting in the waiting room.

Dan comes out, dressed in hospital blues. He looks exhausted.

Jana and Alex hurry over to him.

JANA
Well?

ALEX
Well?

DAN
...Well. I am delighted to say...
(he smiles)
...You have a baby sister.

Dan grins. Jana hugs him.

ALEX
Are you happy Dad?

DAN
Yeah. I'm psyched.

Alex and Dan smile at each other.

EXT. BEACH - DAY

Carter runs in place.

At first, it is framed to look as if Carter is jogging on a treadmill in front of his TV again.

A cell phone rings.

CARTER
Hello? Hey, Dan! Oh my God!
That's great! Got a name yet?
(beat)
That's fantastic. What?
(pause)
No, that's because I'm jogging.

Carter jogs away from the camera, revealing he is on a beach.

CARTER
No, I'm outside. I'm actually
jogging...outside.

Carter jogs off down the beach. His conversation continues as music rises.

THE END.

Dan Foreman (Dennis Quaid, left) and his boss, Carter Duryea (Topher Grace).

Scarlett Johansson (as Alex Foreman) and writer/director/producer Paul Weitz on the set.

Dennis Quaid (right) as Dan Foreman and Topher Grace as Carter Duryea.

Dan Foreman (Dennis Quaid, center) introduces his new boss, Carter Duryea (Topher Grace), to his wife, Ann (Marg Helgenberger).

Dan Foreman (Dennis Quaid, left) and his boss, Carter Duryea (Topher Grace).

Dan Foreman (Dennis Quaid, left) and his boss, Carter Duryea (Topher Grace).

Dan Foreman (Dennis Quaid, left) and his boss, Carter Duryea (Topher Grace).

Carter Duryea (Topher Grace, right) invites himself to have dinner with Dan Foreman (Dennis Quaid) and his family.

Dennis Quaid as Dan Foreman and Scarlett Johansson as his daughter, Alex.

Carter Duryea (Topher Grace) finds himself falling for his employee's daughter, Alex (Scarlett Johansson, seated).

Carter Duryea (Topher Grace) enjoys the company of his employee's daughter, Alex (Scarlett Johansson), a transfer student to NYU.

Dan Foreman (Dennis Quaid) drops off his daughter, Alex (Scarlett Johansson), at NYU.

Dennis Quaid (left) as Dan Foreman and Topher Grace as Carter Duryea.

Carter Duryea (Topher Grace)and Alex Foreman (Scarlett Johansson) walk in New York.

Carter Duryea (Topher Grace) is captivated by Alex (Scarlett Johansson).

Writer/director/producer Paul Weitz (right) and producer Chris Weitz on the set of *In Good Company*.

Dan Foreman (Dennis Quaid) is 51 and his life is good...on the whole. The long-term head of ad sales at the weekly *Sports America* has just celebrated the magazine's biggest year, thanks in large part to Dan's warm, honest, handshake-deal style and the departmental *esprit de corps* he fosters. Even the news of his wife's unexpected pregnancy and the acceptance of his eldest daughter, Alex (Scarlett Johansson), into tony (not to mention expensive) NYU leave Dan happy, though not entirely unconcerned about family finances. He will, as he always has, manage.

Carter Duryea (Topher Grace) is 26 and thinks his life is awesome, mostly. The whiz kid has been devoting himself single-mindedly to getting ahead at the multinational conglomerate Globecom. Management even knows his name—Carter is being "groomed" for his next rung on the corporate ladder: heading up ad sales at one of the cornerstone publications newly acquired by Globecom in their latest takeover, the magazine *Sports America.* Unfortunately for Carter, his promotion coincides with the crumbling of his seven-month marriage and he has no one, save a pet fish, to share his joy with. But he knows he's on his way, he's going places—and he'll manage.

Dan's exasperation at his demotion is nothing compared to his incredulity at being replaced by the 26-year-old Carter. Given his new boss's age and relative experience in ad sales (none), Dan has little desire to be Carter's "wing man." But in light of the new developments at home, he needs his job as much as Carter needs his. Forging a tenuous relationship out of corporate necessity, the two begin working together to meet Globecom's mandate of cutting the department's budget while increasing revenue by 35 percent.

Carter's zeal to deliver to upper management doesn't win him many fans in the *Sports America* offices. His bottom line–focused approach, somewhat lacking in the human side of business, is often at odds with Dan and his devotion to his staff. As Dan sees it, these people are a family—something Carter is sorely lacking. The new department head's loneliness even prompts him to call a Sunday staff meeting and then invite himself to Dan's home for dinner with the Foremans, where Carter and Alex have a chance to talk while Alex whups her dad's boss at foosball.

Later, when the lonely ad salesman runs across the equally lonely NYU transfer student at a Manhattan cafe, the chance meeting rekindles the sparks initially felt at the family dinner...sparks that begin an affair, which the pair find themselves hiding from Dan. The corporate handbook has precious little to say about sleeping with your employee's collegiate daughter, and if word were ever to get out, news of their affair would seriously threaten Carter's détente with Dan, Alex's close relationship with her father, and the progress the two salesmen have made at *Sports America.*

All in all, life for both Dan and Carter just got a bit more complicated.

From the co-director and Academy Award®-nominated co-screenwriter of *About a Boy*, Paul Weitz, comes the insightful and human comedy *In Good Company*. Weitz directs from his own screenplay and produces alongside his brother, Oscar®-nominated filmmaker Chris Weitz (*About a Boy*, *American Pie*). In addition to Quaid, Johansson and Grace, the film stars Marg Helgenberger (*Erin Brokovich*, television's *CSI: Crime Scene Investigation*) as Dan's wife, Ann; and veteran character actors David Paymer (*State and Main*, *Mr. Saturday Night*) and Philip Baker Hall (*Bruce Almighty*, *Magnolia*) as *Sports America* ad salesman Morty and sporting goods business owner Eugene Kalb, respectively.

Joining Weitz behind the camera are executive producers Rodney Liber (*Big Momma's House*) and Andrew Miano (the upcoming *His Dark Materials: The Golden Compass*); director of photography Remi Adefarasin (*About a Boy* and *Elizabeth*); production designer William Arnold (*Shopgirl*); editor Myron Kerstein (*Garden State*); costume designer Molly Maginnis (*Life as a House*); and composer Stephen Trask (*The Station Agent*). Kerry Kohansky serves as co-producer.

THE SYNERGY BEHIND *IN GOOD COMPANY*

Director Paul Weitz is admittedly drawn to material that examines life's surprises, ironies, and coincidences, which he, along with his brother and collaborator, Chris Weitz, successfully explored with their Academy Award®-nominated screen adaptation of Nick Hornby's *About a Boy* (which they also co-directed).

Intrigued by the nontraditional father/son relationship, illustrated in the drama-with-comedy *About a Boy* and earlier in the comedy-with-heart *American Pie* (his directorial debut with Chris), Weitz, who wrote the original script for *In Good Company*, returns to that premise...but with a different, albeit compelling, set of circumstances.

The ever-changing economic landscape of corporate mergers, failing dot-coms, and global conglomerates that has dominated the news over the past several years proved to be the perfect chaotic world in which to set his screenplay.

Says Paul Weitz, "In approaching *In Good Company*, I really wanted to attempt a film in the vein of Billy Wilder, which in some ways *About a Boy* had been. *About a Boy* was such an English film, though, and I now wanted to approach particularly American myths and look at, to some extent, how economic trends affect individual lives. Wilder was able to balance cynicism and optimism, particularly with films like *The Apartment*—he really captured the collision of the American dream and our tendency towards career ambition and how that balances with being a human. And that's something that's still very much present in our landscape today."

After almost six months of refining and researching his initial idea for the screenplay and conferring with his brother Chris (who serves as a producer on the film), Paul had fashioned a very human story of the unlikely relationship between two men who find their satisfying, status quo existences disrupted by the startling truth that they no longer have any control over both the professional and personal sides of their lives. In the process, Weitz had artfully tapped into the emotional and economic zeitgeist that resounded with a multitude of people—the prevailing sentiment that, in this new world order of huge multinational corporations, nearly everyone has a story of a family member or friend who has been displaced, downsized, or affected in some capacity...looking at a now common-place national occurrence, the filmmaker had found a human story.

Weitz notes: "People related stories to me about relatives and friends, in mid-life, being fired or falling victim to corporate downsizing. And now these 50-somethings were looking for a job at a time when they had hoped to be hitting their stride, with plenty of work years left, or retraining to try to enter the workforce in a different line of work. All of that fed my idea about a 51-year-old suddenly finding himself, because of a takeover, the employee of a guy half his age and having to deal with the humiliation of that situation."

But in typical Weitz fashion, the exploration of what could be a bleak turn in a character's life—treading prudently in new corporate terrain in hopes of keeping his job—is handled with gentle and character-driven humor. "Much like in Chekov, I find that anything that's at all serious, the way people usually deal with challenges in life is to laugh about them...if they're healthy at all. I don't find a separation between 'drama' and 'comedy,' it's really a question of the modulation of the comedy."

For Chris Weitz, he found his usual working dynamic with his brother altered for this film. Chris Weitz: "Paul was really intent on telling this story, set in a world of downsizing and synergy as larger corporations take over smaller ones and control of people's lives. My first role was as his sounding board for ideas and sort of encourage him during the writing process. Actually being less involved on this project has been a bit of a blessing for me—the stress has been much lower! I've gotten to let a lot more of the day-to-day decisions go to Paul."

The role of Dan Foreman is one that is tailor-made for Dennis Quaid, who inherently brings a confident, straightforward presence, coupled with a subtle emotional depth to each role he plays. He was the first actor cast in the film and admittedly the anchor for the project's core relationship.

Weitz on Quaid: "I think it's really cool that Dennis—who's still doing action movies and very much a leading man—was willing to take on the role of Dan. Some actors would think it would make them less viable. But what I think really works is that here is a character who is in danger of being sidelined who is still relatively young and incredibly vital. It's more interesting to see that kind of man being pushed aside. I'm lucky Dennis was willing to play one year older than he really is—every day, we had to assiduously put gray in his hair. I should have just given him some of mine."

Chris Weitz adds, "Dennis brings a square-jawed, American straightforwardness to the role just by his very presence."

Casting the youthful-looking and athletic Quaid in the role of a paunchy 51-year-old businessman with salt-and-pepper hair took some imagination. But with help from his hair stylist administering daily applications of gray hair color and costume designer Molly Maginnis (*As Good as It Gets*) utilizing creative wardrobe styling, he was aged up to personify his middle-aged character. "This character is not so much older than myself, so I take solace in the fact that they had to age me up to play him," says Quaid with a laugh. "I'm just glad I'm old enough to play him. I love the part."

For Quaid, the appeal of the project lay with Weitz and his smartly written, relatable, multi-dimensional script. He remarks, "Paul is one of the most talented directors out there...not too many people can do comedy like this...it's very human and intimate. I worked with Mike Nichols about 15 years ago [on *Postcard From the Edge*, opposite Meryl Streep] and he reminds me of Mike.

"What's also great," continues Quaid, "is that Paul really fosters a collaborative process on the set. Some writer/directors are really sticklers about their words, but for Paul, it's really about the process of discovery, even for himself."

Weitz adds, "Dennis has been doing this for such a long time that he is a natural film actor and extremely subtle. Sometimes I knew what he was doing was working in the scene, but I'm never closer than 10 feet away when shooting, so I couldn't tell exactly what he was doing in extreme close-ups. It was only after I was sitting in the editing room that I saw all of the little things that he was doing. He's one of these actors who make things look as effortless as possible, and I think a lot of those actors are overlooked, because their strength is not calling out that they're giving this great performance. They're actually making tons of decisions that are making the character real."

Both Topher Grace and Scarlett Johansson are in agreement with Quaid when it comes to the writer/director, who often was just as collaborative with them when it came to improvising or reworking their dialogue.

Notes Grace, "I'm somewhat new to the game, but I believe the whole point of it is to work with great directors. It's such a director's medium. I've never worked with a writer/director who had written something that wasn't adapted and it's been a total plus. Paul is so open, yet has such a specific idea of what he wants. He is a fascinating guy to be around."

Says Johansson, "Paul is one of the most inspiring directors I've ever worked with; he's so excited about improv and getting new ideas. It's definitely been to our benefit as actors, and his script—it's a perfect little gem, all the characters are so incredibly developed. No matter what story he's telling, it's very real."

Topher Grace is probably best known for his starring role in the hit comedy series *That '70s Show*, but it was his first film role in Steven Soderbergh's Oscar®-nominated film *Traffic* that resonated with the filmmakers when envisioning an actor to portray Carter Duryea. Grace's ability to imbue that character with an edgy intelligence coupled with impeccable comedic timing made for an easy casting decision for Weitz's ambitious young MBA, whose personal life begins to fall apart as he is granted the promotion of his dreams.

Says the director, "Topher has such a great energy, which is very different from Dennis's, which made for a great contrast in the central relationship. I actually did something after their very first rehearsal, which in retrospect could have been disastrous. We read through a scene and then I said to Topher, 'Okay, I'd like you to give some notes to Dennis.' And Topher said, 'Are you kidding me?' 'No, I'm serious.' I was thinking at the time that since the script calls for the younger guy to order the older guy around, I thought it would be interesting to see what would happen there and about the actors' dynamics.

"What I ended up learning first and foremost about Topher is that he's very smart. He said, 'Well, I'm not going to do that.' And they both sort of laughed about it. But Topher made the absolute right decision. Both actors were smart enough to help me avoid a bad start as their director."

"He reminds us most of a young Jack Lemmon," adds Chris Weitz, "in terms of the boyish enthusiasm that he can bring to even the most cynical of characters. He was one of our easiest casting assignments."

"I think when somebody gives a really good performance, one tends to think that they're exactly like their character. Neither Dennis nor Topher is particularly like the character they're playing and yet they both inhabit these guys fully, which I think speaks highly of their acting ability. And they're just great together," comments Paul.

Grace, who filmed *In Good Company* while on hiatus from his popular television series, is emerging as a talented film actor with diverse roles in such divergent projects as as *Win a Date with Tad Hamilton* and *P.S.*, opposite Laura Linney. Grace treats each new film role as an ongoing tutorial and was enthusiastic about working so closely with Quaid: "To be able to work every day for three months with someone as accomplished as Dennis…it's the best graduate school ever. I observe him a lot, and he doesn't talk down to me nearly as much as he should," Grace says with a laugh, "which is nice."

Quaid was equally impressed with his young co-star's ability to deliver when faced with some of Weitz's emotionally complex and lengthy dialogue. "Topher is very talented—I'm amazed by actors who come out of situational comedy. He knows how to make dialogue work. He sucks it in, throws it out and makes it work. He has nailed some pretty substantial scenes with a lot of difficult dialogue with precision."

The role of Alex, Dan and Ann's eldest daughter, who strikes out on her own and subsequently engages in a secret liaison with her dad's young boss, immediately garnered Johansson's attention. At 19 years of age, she saw similarities between herself and the character and felt that, following more than a year of working on back-to-back dramas, a comedy—particularly one with which she had such an affinity—would be the perfect follow-up project.

"Alex resonated with me," remarks Johansson. "We're the same age and a lot of what she's going through—moving out and trying to figure out what she really wants to do—is something that I went through not too long ago. It's a good fit."

To the filmmaker's luck, they signed the young actress prior to what they refer to as "Scarlett Fever," the release and subsequent onslaught of critical acclaim and accolades she received for her performances in *Lost in Translation* and *Girl with a Pearl Earring.*

"We're very inquisitive when it comes to casting," says Chris Weitz. "We see who we want and really go after it intently. It's kind of like we're building a baseball team. We go after our free agents and Scarlett, for instance, was a key acquisition. She's extraordinarily natural and brings a voracity to everything that she does, which is why she's gotten so much acclaim."

Quaid, a veteran actor who has seen firsthand the glare of the media spotlight, states in his own forthright manner, "Scarlett is an incredible actress. You can be the darling of the media but if you haven't got the goods, you haven't got the goods—but she's definitely got the goods."

"I was lucky to cast Scarlett in that she makes the character incredibly real," notes the director. "I like the idea of portraying a relationship in which the conflicts were coming not from dysfunction, but from both the father and the daughter being truly functional and having genuine love for each other. They are in the process of redefining their relationship, with Alex moving away from being her dad's best buddy to this independent and adult woman."

A further testament to the caliber of Weitz's script and reputation as a talented director is the stellar roster of actors the filmmakers assembled for supporting roles: Marg Helgenberger, cast as Ann, Dan's pregnant wife (who simultaneously filmed her role while taping her top-rated television series, *CSI);* David Paymer (*Get Shorty*) as less-than-optimistic *Sports America* ad salesman Morty; Philip Baker Hall (*Bruce Almighty*) as sports equipment company owner Eugene Kalb; Clark Gregg (*The Human*

Stain) as driven Globecom management team member Steckle; Selma Blair (*Hellboy*) as Carter's short-term wife, Kimberly; and Malcolm McDowell (*A Clockwork Orange*) as the enigmatic and charismatic chairman of Globecom, Teddy K.

Helgenberger's affection for the script, the cast and the filmmakers is evident when she says, "It's such a wonderfully calibrated script, with the juxtaposition of Dan's work life and his family life. Paul's script is warm and funny and observant, and he's come up with a really timely American story to tell. But he doesn't hit you over the head with the age issues—he really comes at it from a comedic perspective, which is a much more subtle way to approach the themes in the story. Dennis is such a pro and the rest of the cast are just marvelous to work with. It's projects like this that really attract me to working in film. There is so much heart and soul in this."

★ ★ ★

Principal photography commenced in mid-March, filming in and around the Los Angeles, including: suburban Pasadena, filming interiors and exteriors of the Foreman home; and downtown Los Angeles, which provided not only the urban backdrop for several scenes, but also the sound stages, which housed the impressive 6,000-square-foot sets that comprised the various work spaces within the *Sports America* high-rise offices.

Production designer William Arnold and his art department spent close to three months designing, constructing and dressing the modern glass—accented *Sports America* set, which is elevated six feet above the ground allowing an expansive view of the New York skyline (courtesy of a 25' high, 211' long trans light, ostensibly an enlarged color transparency) surrounding portions of the set. Specifically challenging to Arnold was having to create a practical way to transform the existing set into two additional and differing *Sport America* offices, as the company falls victim to the takeover and the subsequent shifts in personnel affect the workspace—which was accomplished by utilizing a second trans light with an alternate city view and by reconfiguring walls and re-dressing the cavernous sets, courtesy of set decorator, David Smith.

Once filming began, it was Chris Weitz who found himself in unfamiliar territory as he watched his brother take on the sole directing duties. "I get a lot less respect on set now," he quips, "I feel like the trophy wife who's hanging around and people feel they have to talk to."

But Chris, who is set to make his own solo directorial debut with the upcoming *His Dark Materials: The Golden Compass*, is quite serious when speaking of his brother and his strengths as a director: "Paul is fantastic when it comes to working with actors. He comes from a theater background and really has a deep understanding and love for what an actor does when he or she goes about performing a scene."

Executive producer Andrew Miano echoes that sentiment, adding, "One of the things that actors respond to is the chance to take on a part that both challenges them and allows them to change it up a bit...I believe that's what attracts actors to Paul. He is very good at giving them an opportunity to shine."

Weitz, however, has not forsaken his theater roots. He recently returned to the New York stage, writing the dark comedy *Roulette*, which premiered in February 2004 (while he was in pre-production on the film) at the prestigious Ensemble Studio Theatre, where he has been a member since 1993. He has written and directed numerous theatrical productions including *Mango Tea* and *All for One*, which starred Calista Flockhart and Liev Schreiber. His play, *Privilege,* will be produced by The Second Stage Theatre in 2005.

Part of the challenge for three of Weitz's stars lay in the physical (i.e. athletic) demands called for in the script. To prepare for her role as a talented sportswoman, Johansson began training with tennis pro/consultant Nels Van Patten beginning in January 2004 and, to her credit, kept up with her weekly lessons during the grueling schedule of awards shows, events and premieres surrounding the blitz around the releases of both *Lost in Translation* and *Girl with a Pearl Earring.*

"I'm a New York City girl and I've never held a tennis racquet in my life. But that's one of the perks of this profession, you get opportunities to learn new things and Nels has made me so enthusiastic about the sport."

Quaid and Grace also had to prepare for their share of athletic challenges, particularly with the film's key basketball scene, where the ad sales team takes on management in a "friendly" game—with management being so friendly they recruit from other departments, like shipping and receiving.

Quaid, who has previously starred in several sports-driven films, acknowledged that basketball is not his strong suit. Grace also admits to struggling a bit with the scenes as well: "I'm not a very good basketball player…it was definitely a lot of takes until we'd sink a shot. But the good news is Dennis is worse than I am, so I didn't feel too bad," he adds with a grin.

Cast and crew spent eight weeks filming in Los Angeles before relocating to New York City for a week, to capture the unique exteriors of Manhattan's Madison Square Garden, Washington Square Park, Chinatown, TriBeCa, and NYU.

As the end of filming neared, it is safe to say—starting from Weitz's early musings on his screenplay and ending with the last shot filmed on location at New York's Madison Square Garden—that the hard work of 35 different departments comprised of several hundred people on both coasts truly embodied the all-encompassing philosophies mantraed by the Globecom employees in the screenplay. As Teddy K might say, "Good synergy."

CAST AND CREW CREDITS

UNIVERSAL PICTURES Presents

A DEPTH OF FIELD Production

A PAUL WEITZ Film

DENNIS QUAID TOPHER GRACE SCARLETT JOHANSSON

IN GOOD COMPANY

MARG HELGENBERGER DAVID PAYMER CLARK GREGG

PHILIP BAKER HALL FRANKIE FAISON TY BURRELL

KEVIN CHAPMAN AMY AQUINO ZENA GREY

Casting by
JOSEPH MIDDLETON, C.S.A.

Original Score by
STEPHEN TRASK

Associate Producers
MATT EDDY
LAWRENCE PRESSMAN

Co-Producer
KERRY KOHANSKY

Costume Designer
MOLLY MAGINNIS

Editor
MYRON KERSTEIN

Production Designer
WILLIAM ARNOLD

Director of Photography
REMI ADEFARASIN, B.S.C.

Executive Producers
RODNEY LIBER
ANDREW MIANO

Produced by
PAUL WEITZ and
CHRIS WEITZ

Written and Directed by
PAUL WEITZ

CAST

Dan . . . . Dennis Quaid
Carter . . . . Topher Grace
Alex . . . . Scarlett Johansson
Ann . . . . Marg Helgenberger
Morty . . . . David Paymer
Steckle . . . . Clark Gregg
Eugene Kalb . . . . Philip Baker Hall
Kimberly . . . . Selma Blair
Corwin . . . . Frankie Faison
Enrique Colon . . . . Ty Burrell
Lou . . . . Kevin Chapman
Alicia . . . . Amy Aquino
Jana . . . . Zena Grey
Receptionist . . . . Colleen Camp
Obstetrician . . . . Lauren Tom
Porsche Dealer . . . . Ron Bottitta
Waiter . . . . Jon Collin
Maitre d' . . . . Shishir Kurup
Theo . . . . Tim Edward Rhoze
Hector . . . . Enrique Castillo
Petey . . . . John Cho
Young Executive . . . . Chris Ausnit
Loan Officer . . . . Francesca P. Roberts
Lawyer . . . . Gregory North
Moving Men . . . . Gregory Hinton
Todd Lyon
Thomas J. Dooley
Basketball Ringer . . . . Robin Kirksey
Maya (Roommate) . . . . Kate Ellis
Carter's Assistant . . . . Nick Schutt
Salesmen . . . . John Kepley
Mobin Khan
Saleswoman . . . . Jeanne Kort
Mike . . . . Dean A. Parker
Fired Employees . . . . Richard Hotson
Shar Washington
Teddy K's Assistant . . . . Rebecca Hedrick
Globecom Technician . . . . Miguel Arteta
Kid at Party . . . . Sam Tippe
Anchorwoman . . . . Roma Torre
Legally Dedd . . . . Andre Cablayan
Dante Powell

CREW

Unit Production Manager. . . . . Dustin Bernard
First Assistant Director . . . . Richard Graves
Second Assistant Director. . . . . Eric Sherman
Stunt Coordinator . . . . Ernie Orsatti
Stunt Players. Stanton Barrett
David Hugghins
Michael Hugghins
Anthony Kramme
Art Director. . . . . Sue Chan
Set Decorator . . . . David Smith
Chief Lighting Technician . . . . Colin Campbell
Key Grip . . . . Jeff Case
Sound Mixer . . . . David Wyman
Script Supervisor. . . . . Alicia Accardo
Location Manager . . . . Colleen Hilary Gibbons
Costume Supervisor . . . . Sandy Kenyon
Makeup Department Head. . . . . Nena Smarz
Hair Department Head . . . . Barbara Olvera
Production Coordinator . . . . M. Michelle Nishikawa
Accountant . . . . Paul Belenardo
Transportation Coordinators . . . . Gary Shephard
Larry Shephard
Construction Coordinator . . . . Robert Carlyle
Property Master. . . . . Todd Ellis
Special Effects Supervisor . . . . John Hartigan
Post Production Supervisor . . . . . Virginia Landis Albertson
A Camera Operator . . . . Ray De La Motte
B Camera/Steadicam Operator . . . . P. Scott Sakamoto
First Assistant A Camera . . . . Dennis Seawright
First Assistant B Camera . . . . Michael Endler
Second Assistant A Camera. . . . . Shawn Landis
Second Assistant B Camera. . . . . Kevin De La Motte
Loader . . . . Mike Cahoon
Still Photographer . . . . Glen Wilson
Unit Publicist . . . . Carol McConnaughey
Boom Operator. . . . . Earl Sampson
Sound Utility. Chet Leonard
Video Assist . . . . Jay Huntoon
24 FPS Playback. Steve Irwin
Best Boy Electric. . . . . Eric Bernstein
Lamp Operators. . . . . Sean Smith
Ian Strang
Rigging Gaffer . . . . Ray Gonzales
Best Boy Rigging Electric . . . . Russell Ayer
Best Boy Grip . . . . Tom Greene
Dolly Grips . . . . Chris Scurria
Chuck Crivier
Grips . . . . Chris Conahan
Scott Eades
Carlos Gallardo
Greg Romero
Kat Bueno
Key Rigging Grip. Bret Rubin
Best Boy Rigging Grip . . . . Scott Jackson
Rigging Grips . . . . Mark Elias
Mark Rubin
Steve Suveg
Justin Van Fleet
Assistant Location Managers. . . . . Leann Emmert
Albert Salsich
Locations Assistant. . . . . Glen Evans
Transportation Captain . . . . Kenny Youngblood
1st Assistant Editor. . . . . Greg Thompson
Assistant Editor-Avid . . . . Rachel Goodlett
Assistant Editors . . . . Marisa Morabito
Jim Makiej
Editorial PA. . . . . Matt Maddox
Key Costumers . . . . Reese Spensley
Danielle Baker
Sally Smith-McCardle
Sharon Lynch
Makeup Artist. Tricia Sawyer
Hair Stylists. . . . . Laine Trzinski
Michelle Elam
Jo Jo Gerard
Hair Stylist for Mr. Quaid. . . . . Kelly Nelson
Makeup Artist for Mr. Quaid. . . . . Ron Berkeley
Assistant Property Master. . . . . Tim Wetzel
Property Assistant . . . . Allison Gross
Special Effects Foreman . . . . Ron Roseguard
Lead Man . . . . Richard Brunton
Set Designer . . . . Liz Lapp
On Set Dresser . . . . Keith Sale
Drapery Foreman . . . . Ruben Abarca
Set Dressers . . . . Billy Baker
Michael Brogan
Brenner Harris
Peter Kang
Eric Kelly
Thierry Labbe
Richard Stockton
Sammy Tell
Darrell Vangilder
Buyer . . . . Kristen Gassner
Graphic Designer . . . . Adam Khalid
Art Department Coordinator. . . . . Christina Rollo
General Foreman. . . . . Jamie Orendorff
Construction Foreman . . . . W. Scott Mason
Propmaker Foreman. . . . . Jimmy Flores
Paint Foreman . . . . Gerald Gates
Labor Foreman . . . . Johnny Morales
Plaster Foreman . . . . Eugenio Quintero
Greens Foreman. . . . . Steven Miller
Standby Painter . . . . Alexa Shushan
Labor Gang Bosses. . . . . Gilberto Gastelum
Manny Hernandez
Chris Revuelta

Paint Gang Bosses . . . . Gary Antonacci
Tim Lehman
Propmaker Gang Bosses . . . . James Arrigo
Craig Bernatzke
Ken Keavy
Gary Stel
2nd 2nd Assistant Director . . . . Jodi Lowry Fisher
Additional 2nd Assistant Director . . . . . . Dominick Scarola
Assistant Production Coordinator . . . . Ray Utarnachitt
Production Secretary . . . . Frank Inserra
1st Assistant Accountant . . . . Edna Wilkerson
2nd Assistant Accountant . . . . Karen Shane
Payroll Accountant . . . . John Montgomery
Construction Accountant . . . . Charlie Araki
Accounting Clerk . . . . Steve Golebiowski
Assistant to Paul Weitz . . . . Monique Ramirez
Assistant to Chris Weitz . . . . Marc Hofstatter
Assistant to Rodney Liber . . . . Rebecca Hedrick
Production Assistants . . . . Jonas Spaccarotelli
Matt Rawls
Audrey Clark
Matt Ferrell
Sean Jennings
Taylor Roberts
Gary Williams
Shaun O'Banion
Louie Giangrande
Liam Cassidy
Nicolas Lazareff
Casting Associates . . . . Kathleen Tomasik
Lauren Grey
Rachel Tenner
Extras Casting . . . . Background Players
Judy Cook
Stand-In for Mr. Quaid . . . . Tom Dooley
Stand-In for Mr. Grace . . . . Alan Charles
Stand-In for Ms. Johansson . . . . Heather Berrett
Catering . . . . Mario's Catering
Craft Service . . . . Rich Cody
Medics . . . . B.J. Smith
Ken Clark
Projectionists . . . . Michael Testa
Tommy Dickson
Studio Teacher . . . . Carol Gans
Police Coordinator . . . . Myron Biting
Security Coordinator . . . . Richard Lopez, Sr.
Basketball Consultant . . . . Stephen Thompson
Tennis Consultant . . . . Nels Van Patten
Tennis Double . . . . Jordana Kono
Supervising Sound Editor . . . . Eric Warren Lindemann
Sound Effects Editors . . . . Richard Adrian, M.P.S.E.
Bryan Watkins
Ben Wilkins
Supervising Dialogue Editor . . . . . . Stephanie Flack, M.P.S.E.

Dialogue Editor . . . . James Morioka
ADR Editor . . . . Kimberly Lowe Voigt, M.P.S.E.
Foley Editor . . . . Valerie Davidson
1st Assistant Sound Editor . . . . Nancy Barker, M.P.S.E.
Assistant Sound Editors . . . . Nathan Whitehead
Paul Hackner
Re-Recording Mixers . . . . John Reitz
Dave Campbell
Gregg Rudloff
Recordists . . . . Mark Johnston
Mike Jimenez
Foley Artists . . . . John Roesch
Alyson Moore
Mary Jo Lang
Scott Morgan
ADR Mixer . . . . Thomas J. O'Connell
ADR Recordist . . . . Rick Canelli
ADR Voice Casting . . . . Barbara Harris
ADR Voices . . . . Jason Broad
Judi Durand
Greg Finley
Arlin Miller
Vernon Scott
Sound Coordinator . . . . Matt Hedges
Supervising Music Editor . . . . Charles Martin Inouye
Music Scoring Mixer . . . . Bobby Fernandez
Executive in Charge of Music for
Universal Pictures . . . . Kathy Nelson
Orchestration . . . . Damon Intrabartolo
Music Recordist . . . . Robert Fernandez
Music Contractor . . . . Debbi Datz-Pyle
Pre-Recorded & Mixed by . . . . Tim O'Heir
Music Preparation . . . . Julian Bratolyubov
Pre-Recorded at . . . . Signet Sound
Orchestra Recorded at . . . . 20th Century Fox
Score Mixed at . . . . Scream Studio
Main Title Design by . . . . Picture Mill
End Titles and Opticals by . . . . Pacific Title
Optical Sound Negative by . . . . N.T. Audio
Negative Cutter . . . . Mo Henry
Color Timer . . . . Chris De Laguardia
DTS Consultants . . . . John Keating
Dan Victor
Camera Dollies by . . . . Chapman /
Leonard Studios Equipment, Inc.
Cameras Supplied by . . . . Otto Nemenz

New York Unit

Unit Production Manager . . . . Jonathan Filley
Second Assistant Director . . . . Michelle Keiser
Location Manager . . . . Santiago Quinones
Asst. Location Managers . . . . Joaquin Diego Prange
Cesar Quinones
Production Coordinator . . . . Drew Tidwell

Asst. Production Coordinator . . . . Andrea Pappas
Art Director . . . . Fred Kolo
Costume Supervisors . . . . Chuck Crutchfield
Susan Wright
Chief Lighting Technician . . . . Clay Liversidge
Best Boy Electric. . . . . Bill Almeida
Key Grip . . . . Richard Guinness, Jr.
Best Boy Grip . . . . James Scutakes
Dolly Grips . . . . Danny Beaman
Jasper Johnson
Video Assist . . . . Joel Holland
Key Hairstylist . . . . Donna Marie Fischetto
Key Make Up Artist . . . . Nuria Sitja
Property Master . . . . Michael Saccio
Leadman . . . . Joe Proscia
Transportation Captain. . . . . John Leonidas
Transportation Co-Captain. . . . . Gene O'Neill
Production Secretary. . . . . Scott Sullens
Assistant Accountants. . . . . Jean Kalanzi
Kelly O'Bier

SOUNDTRACK ON HOLLYWOOD RECORDS

"GLASS, CONCRETE & STONE"
Written by David Byrne
Performed by David Byrne
Courtesy of Nonesuch Records
By arrangement with Warner Strategic Marketing

"SISTER SURROUND"
Written by Torbjorn Lundberg, Mattias Barjed, Karl Ake Gustafsson, Christian Person, Fredrik Sandsten, Martin Hederos
Performed by The Soundtrack Of Our Lives
Courtesy of Universal Records
Under license from Universal Music Enterprises
and
Courtesy of Warner Music Sweden AB
By arrangement with Warner Strategic Marketing

"GONE FOR GOOD"
Written by James R. Mercer
Performed by The Shins
Courtesy of Sub Pop Records

"NAKED AS WE CAME"
Written by Sam Beam
Performed by Iron & Wine
Courtesy of Sub Pop Records

"GET WIT ME"
Written by Fred Wreck and Dante Powell
Performed by Fred Wreck and Dante Powell

"CHAIN OF FOOLS"
Written by Donald Covay
Performed by Aretha Franklin
Courtesy of Atlantic Recording Corp.
By arrangement with Warner Strategic Marketing

"SUNSET SOON FORGOTTEN "
Written by Sam Beam
Performed by Iron & Wine
Courtesy of Sub Pop Records

"CANNONBALL "
Written by Damien Rice
Performed by Damien Rice
Courtesy of Vector Recordings LLC / Warner Bros. Records, Inc., 14th Floor Records
By arrangement with Warner Strategic Marketing and Warner Strategic Marketing UK

"BESAME MUCHO"
Written by Consuelo Velazquez
Performed by Diana Krall
Courtesy of The Verve Music Group
Under license from Universal Music Enterprises

"TEN YEARS AHEAD"
Written by Torbjorn Lundberg, Mattias Barjed, Karl Ake Gustafsson, Christian Person, Fredrik Sandsten, Martin Hederos
Performed by The Soundtrack Of Our Lives
Courtesy of Universal Records
Under license from Universal Music Enterprises
and
Courtesy of Warner Music Sweden AB
By arrangement with Warner Strategic Marketing

"THOSE TO COME"
Written by James R. Mercer
Performed by The Shins
Courtesy of Sub Pop Records

"REELING IN THE YEARS"
Written by Walter Becker, Donald Fagen
Performed by Steely Dan
Courtesy of MCA Records
Under license from Universal Music Enterprises

"SOLSBURY HILL"
Written and Performed by Peter Gabriel
Peter Gabriel appears courtesy of Real World Records Ltd./ Virgin Records Ltd and Geffen Records

"THE TRAPEZE SWINGER"
Written by Sam Beam
Performed by Iron & Wine
Courtesy of Sub Pop Records

The NY1 logo is a registered trademark.

All trademarks and copyrights of the National Hockey League and its Member Teams are used with permission. All rights reserved.

The Major League Baseball trademarks depicted in this motion picture were licensed by Major League Baseball Properties, Inc.

Stock images courtesy of Icon Sports Media Inc.

Stock images courtesy of Getty Images.

Stock images courtesy of Corbis.

Special Thanks to

Madison Square Garden

City of Pasadena Film Office, Ariel Penn

EIDC / Los Angeles Film Office
Jodi Strong, Director of Operations

Porsche Cars North America

Peter Kellner

Patricia Weitz

Color by TECHNICOLOR
KODAK Motion Picture Film
DTS®
SDDS
Dolby Digital
Certificate # 41265
IATSE
MPAA Logo

MPAA Code Classification: **PG-13**

About the Writer/Director

Director/Writer/Producer **Paul Weitz** co-directed the award-winning hit *About a Boy*, with his brother and frequent collaborator, Chris Weitz, also adapting the screenplay from Nick Hornby's novel. The screenplay received an Academy Award® nomination for Best Adapted Screenplay, as well as similar nominations from BAFTA, Writers Guild, Chicago Film Critics and Humanitas; the film was named one of the AFI's Movies of the Year and was nominated for Golden Globe and Golden Satellite awards for Best Comedy, winning Best Studio Comedy Feature at the U.S. Comedy Arts Festival.

In 1999, Paul and Chris Weitz formed Depth of Field, their Los Angeles-based production company. Their diverse slate of upcoming projects include *A Stolen Life*, a remake of the Bette Davis classic to be directed by Miguel Arteta (*The Good Girl*); the feature adaptation of Michael Moorcock's fantasy epic *The Elric Saga*; the comedies *Army Geek* and *The Last Bachelor Party*; and the WWI drama *Silent Night*.

Weitz made his feature directorial debut teaming with his brother on *American Pie*, the phenomenally successful first installment of the *Pie* franchise.

Prior to their screenwriting work on *About a Boy*, the brothers collaborated on several screenplays, including *Antz*. Weitz also made his acting debut in the Sundance Film Festival hit, *Chuck and Buck*.

Born in New York, Weitz's grandfather was fabled agent Paul Kohner (who represented filmmakers such as John Huston, Billy Wilder and Ingmar Bergman) and his parents are fashion designer/writer John Weitz and Oscar®-nominated actress Susan Kohner.

Weitz graduated from Wesleyan University with a degree in film. His last year there, his play *Mango Tea* was produced off-Broadway with Marisa Tomei and Rob Morrow by New York's Ensemble Studio Theatre. EST also produced his next works, *Captive* and *All for One*, and most recently, the ensemble comedy *Roulette*, starring Larry Bryggman, Anna Paquin, Ana Gasteyer, and Shawn Hatosy (which *The New York Times* cited as an "original jewel"). His play, *Privilege*, will be produced by the Second Stage Theater in 2005.

March 30/07